SETTLED
FURROWS

by

Dorothy Hamilton

HERALD PRESS, SCOTTDALE, PENNSYLVANIA

In Memory of Mercedes

1/

Rachael Brooks was kneeling at the edge of her asparagus bed when she heard the rattling rumble of the loose planks on the Cabin Creek bridge. A car was coming along the Macedonia Pike from the west.

Rachael slid the point of her paring knife below the surface of the mealy soil and severed another tender stalk from the maze of roots. She recalled the day she'd bought a berry box of started asparagus from Neff's Nursery in Mooreland. It'd taken six years for the bed to spread so she could get enough for a meal from one cutting. "And I couldn't now if there was anyone here except me. John dearly loved it with my butter sauce."

The spring air was like silver. Indiana had been resurrected from the frozen tomb of winter. All the trees were leafed out except the hickory across the drive. Now it was sending the tight candles of its budding foliage into the mellow sunshine.

The pear tree at the end of the garden was a giant nosegay of fragrance. Rachael often thought the gnarled tree paid its rent on earth with the loveliness of blossom-

5

ing time. The fruit was hard and knotty and wouldn't cook to a tender state, but the waxy starlike petals were pleasing to the senses of sight and smell.

As Rachael walked toward the garden gate she noticed that the approaching car hadn't come within sight. There were no houses between Brooks farm and the village of Willow Bend. *Maybe someone stopped at the bridge to see if the fish are running in Cabin Creek.*

She was whisking the fragments of soil from her brown oxfords when a voice said, "Pardon me. I hope I didn't frighten you."

Rachael looked toward the corner of the house and saw a tall young man. His black hair shone in the silvery sunshine. *Not from oil. It's just clean.*

"No. I'm not that easily scared," Rachael said. "Especially not in broad daylight."

The man took off his shell-rimmed glasses and walked toward her. The morning sun had glinted on the lens.

"I'm Kenneth Holden," he said. "The new — "

"Oh, the minister," Rachael said. "We've been expecting you."

"Wondering what I'd be like, I imagine."

"Well, yes. That's usual," Rachael said. "You've probably tried to picture us in your mind too. But where'd I mislay my manners! Come on in the house."

"Thank you," Rev. Holden said. "I wish I could. But I had tire trouble back up the street and I'd better get it fixed and get my car out of the way."

He must come from the city, Rachael thought. *Calling a road a street.*

"Is there a garage up in the village?" the minister asked.

6

"Yes. There is. Sam Clinton's place. But he doesn't like to make road calls," Rachael said. "I tell you what! My son David will be along soon. He farms this place and comes here to feed his Shorthorn cattle as regular as clock work. He'll help you and take your tire to Willow Bend in his pickup truck. So you might as well come in a while."

She led the way into the sunny yellow kitchen. "I'll empty my apron of this morning's asparagus crop, then we can find more comfortable chairs in the living room."

"This is fine," the minister said, looking around. His eyes rested first on the potted Jerusalem cherries on the deep windowsill, then on the high-backed rocker with a spray of gold leaves on the black lacquer.

He shook his head when he noticed the gray enamel range with the polished silver trim. "I didn't know people still used wood-burning stoves," he said. "My Aunt Esta had one."

"That's a fraud," Rachael said. "We have a natural gas well and my husband put burners in the firebox. It's not up-to-date in looks, that Home Comfort of mine, but it's cheap fuel and it works fine. Come this way."

During the fifteen minutes before David Brooks' blue pickup truck pulled in the barn lot gate communication of a rare sort was established between the new minister and the first parishioner he'd met. It was in a way acquaintance by osmosis. Neither was uneasy about what to say. Each remark was a revelation of the other's nature.

Rev. Holden looked at the tall sectional bookcases and then around the room before turning to Rachael. He smiled and said, "Another booklover I see."

Rachael nodded. *He sees my open book. And the stack*

on the footstool. He knows they're not for show.

The conversation drifted from books to names of places. "Willow Bend," the young man said. "That's pleasing to the ear. Do willows grow here?"

"Yes, but not so many now. The creek's been dredged and water runs off to White River more quickly. There aren't so many bends."

"Names interest me. I'm always reading signs the few times when I could get out into the country."

"Then you are from the city?" Rachael asked.

"Yes. Detroit. Not so far away. But different," Rev. Holden said.

"I suppose so," Rachael said. "But there are differences here too. Even among people who've lived in Eminence Township all their lives."

"Are you trying to tell me something, Mrs. Brooks?" the minister said. He'd taken off his glasses and was polishing them with a gray-bordered handkerchief.

"Not really," Rachael said. Then she smiled. "I have the feeling that you already know differences exist in congregations. Seminaries are surely aware of that fact."

"They are. But you aren't going to tell me who or what's involved, are you?"

Rachael shook her head. The bun of silver braids on top of her head shifted with her intensity. "No. For more than one reason. First, you'll hear soon enough. Plenty. And from both sides. But I don't participate in side-taking. And I think every new minister should be allowed to come in and see things with his own eyes. But that's not possible — or so it seems."

The room was quiet for a few minutes except for the clicking tick of the walnut-cased clock on the shelf.

Then the new minister drew a deep breath and said, "Thank you."

"For what?" Rachael asked.

"For being here. For offering me an oasis, or a port, or a secret place."

Rachael understood what he meant and she knew that he'd probably need a refuge when he learned of the rift in the Willow Bend congregation. The man before him hadn't been able to settle the quarrel that divided the membership. That's why he resigned. That's why there'd been no preaching services at the red-brick church for seven weeks. They had to wait until a seminary student could arrange to hold a pastorate while he finished his work.

Rachael leaned her head back against the crocheted doily on her rose-colored armchair. "You are always welcome here. To talk or not. To rest or work. Or to pray. Maybe we can be a two-person redemptive group."

The minister settled his glasses and then leaned forward eagerly. "You, too! You believe in the power of such groups?"

"I do," Rachael said. "I've been praying that someone would lead into organizing one here."

"Why not you?" Kenneth Holden asked.

Rachael shook her head. "It's not time. Or I'm not the right one to recognize whether it is or not. But seems like folks, or some anyway, are enjoying the feud. But not me. I'm ready for this one to be settled."

Just then a glint of light flashed across the window. A truck was pulling up to the picket fence separating the yard from the barn lot.

"There's David," Rachael said. "I'd better call to him before he heads toward the feedlot."

After her son had helped the minister on his way, Rachael decided to stir up a batch of oatmeal cookies, a double recipe. She'd try to get some ready for David to take home. It wouldn't be a bad idea to send or take some up to the parsonage. An unmarried man might not do much cooking.

"Of course," Rachael thought, "when Lucy Cavanaugh and Cora Landess find out the new preacher's here they'll run a race to supply him with 'vittles.'"

As she creamed butter and brown sugar, she assessed her impressions of the minister. The first impact was favorable. He'd simply said his name was Kenneth Holden. He hadn't tacked the title on the front. There was something in her that didn't like anything that smacked of being pretentious. Her brother-in-law in Fort Wayne wanted even his family to call him Doctor Wilkins. Once Rachael had said, "Oh, Tom, don't be so uppity. What if I asked you to call me Housewife Rachael or your wife insisted on being Teacher Frances?"

She broke four buff Orpington eggs into the blue bowl and added up what she already knew of Kenneth Holden. He's not snobbish. He's sensitive to people's thoughts. He's aware of the possibility of trouble. But there's something else. What is it? Then she knew. She'd heard a sermon once on the subject of "The Galilean Accent." It dealt with the fact that Christlike tones, thoughts, and convictions should be detected in His followers. "That's it. This young man has the Galilean Accent. This is good."

2/

It was two days before Rachael saw the new minister again. But she heard whisperings and reverberations of evidence that people around Willow Bend knew he'd arrived. The first sign came from the ringing of the telephone.

Four families were on Rachael's side of the multiparty circuit and four on the other. She could hear only the two long, the long and a short, and three short rings. But if she tried to use the phone any one of the other parties might be talking.

Sometimes Rachael wished she could rip the wires out of the neighborhood. This feeling was stronger since Lily Cavanaugh had sent the pot of pink hydrangeas to Connie James' mother. That's when the quarrel sprouted. It had slowly spread from the Women's Circle to a large part of the congregation. Most of the spreading was done over the wires of the Eastern Telephone Company.

"It's a wonder the lines don't crackle and snap or even spark," Tilda Barley had said the day after Rev. Holden arrived. "The anger and spite they carry is enough to short-circuit the switchboard over in Mount Carmel."

Rachael had smiled to herself. Tilda was as good a friend as a person could want. There wasn't an ounce of meanness in her lean frame, but she had the habit of eavesdropping, which was labeled "nibbing" in Willow Bend. Maybe it was because she was lonely. What she heard and often repeated didn't add much to her store of pleasures in life.

The two women were dividing iris roots that day. Tilda lived on the sandy strip beyond the village and had trouble getting things to take root. Every spring Rachael gave her starts to replace what hadn't made it through other winters. She'd divided spicy chrysanthemums, waxy myrtle vines, and lacy maidenhair ferns.

For the last few years Tilda had given more and more space to iris. "It's nigh to impossible to keep them from growing," she said. "And they keep spreading, leaving me less lawn to mow."

Rachael was pushing the spade into the mealy soil. "Here, let me do that," Tilda said. "If I come a-begging the least I can do is dig for myself. Now are you sure you want to spare these purple velvet ones?"

"I'm sure," Rachael said. "See for yourself. They're knobby and humped out of the ground. They'll do better to be divided."

After the roots were dropped into the net onion bag, the two friends went into the kitchen. "I'll make us a cup of tea," Rachael said. "You're not in any hurry to get home, are you?"

"I don't know what for," Tilda said. "I have trouble covering my days with a few chores — now I know what you're thinking. I need to find me something to do with my hands — 'sides scrubbing and scouring."

"Well, you *do*," Rachael said. "There's any number of things you're good at. Like your hooked rugs and the crocheted beads — the seed pearls."

"*Oat* pearls," Tilda said. "Well as a matter of fact I do enjoy seeing wool scraps and tiny little beads turning into something pretty. But why bother? I've loaded you down with the likes. I can't afford to buy much burlap and supplies."

"I know. But I still think plenty of folks would like to have what you make. If we could just think of the right place."

"Well, let me know if you do. I could use the cash. My roof's leaking worse. It took three pans to catch the drips during last Friday night's thunderstorm."

"You make up a rug or two and get some beads ahead," Rachael said. "Let's act on faith, not fear. Maybe a way will open up."

Tilda had smiled and nodded. She told Rachael she was better than sulphur and molasses to the spirits. "Of course, I don't take a tonic but I think I will take your advice. When you get that faith look in your eyes, I know something's likely to happen. What's in your mind? Has that young preacher put something new in your head?"

Rachael told her friend about the visit with Kenneth Holden and about the idea of a redemptive group.

Tilda said it would take a passel of praying to break down the clods of anger between the factions and make the Willow Bend congregation a fertile field again.

"It's like I told you before. The hate's getting stronger and stronger. The things they say on the phone!"

"I can imagine," Rachael said.

After Tilda started up the Macedonia Pike toward home

13

Rachael sat down in her armchair and looked back to the beginning of the split in the church. Actually the pot of pink hydrangeas hadn't caused the fissure. It was just a wedge that widened long-existing feelings and differences.

Rachael ran one finger up and down the soft wales of the corduroy upholstery as she retraced the experiences of the past fifteen months. Certain convictions began to assume clarity in her mind.

If Connie James had been a founding family, had lived in Eminence Township all or most of her life, there'd be no trouble. Then Cora Landess wouldn't have objected, at least not so violently, because Lucy ordered a flower sent to Connie's mother.

Cora wasn't the only person who resented new-comers. Several people called the residents of Candlewood Hills foreigners. They said that the people who bought the split-level homes in the thirty-acre tract were city folks moving out to get away from high taxes, and that they expected farmers' taxes to build schools and hire buses for their kids.

Cora was more bitter than the rest because she and Walter had wanted that thirty acres. As Tilda once said it didn't pour oil on troubled waters for Lucy to be the one to send the hydrangeas to Connie's mother. It was Fred Marsh, Lucy's brother, who'd sold the thirty acres to the land development firm.

So the fissure of difference already existed. But it hadn't widened or deepened for a long time. Life and activities sort of stepped over or bridged the antagonisms and prejudices.

Then little Mrs. Enright had fallen and broken her hip. After a stay in the hospital Connie made plans to have her taken to her home. She'd told Rachael one day at the Women's Circle meeting, "I know it won't be easy. With two little ones there's already plenty to do. But I couldn't bear to *think* of Mamma being in a nursing home. Besides I want her. Want to take care of her. So does Brad. He loves my mother."

The James family had been the first people from Candlewood Hills to come to Willow Bend Church. And for a long time they were the only ones.

Rachael had suggested to the previous minister that this was a possible place to find new members. But she'd never heard whether or not he called on anyone along the curving drives.

She'd even gone so far as to bring the matter up before the official board of the church a time or two. "Perhaps we could have visiting teams, or send welcoming letters along with a church bulletin."

No action was taken. People all glanced Cora's way and then dropped their eyes. Her tight-lipped expression seemed to silence them. Were people cowards or had they foreseen what was happening now? They could have been evading the responsibility for reaching out to pick up the wedge that would split the church.

So Rachael, and sometimes Tilda, had driven over to the subdivision several afternoons. Connie took them to other homes and in a short time six other families began coming to church, not as regularly as the James, but as often as many longtime members and more than some.

Rachael met Connie's mother more than once before she came to convalesce from her fall. She'd learned that Mrs. Enright had been a teacher in a church mission school in Kentucky. She'd asked her to speak at the

Women's Circle meeting the month before she was injured.

So it seemed natural to Rachael, and some of the others, that Lucy as chairman of the Flower Committee send a plant to Mrs. Enright. She'd provided a most interesting program and wouldn't take a cent, not even for the round-trip bus ticket to and from Indianapolis.

Besides that, Connie was now a contributing member of the circle. She'd organized the nursery school for migrant children, the circle's home mission project, overriding some opposition. In fact, before Connie's mother fell there was talk that the lovely and vibrant young mother should be nominated as president of the group.

Looking back Rachael could see that such talk was probably another wedge widening the rift between Cora and Lucy. No one was ever eager or even willing to be head of the circle. No one but Cora, and she'd taken it as often as it was offered. Lucy had served four years to Cora's three.

As all this ran through Rachael's mind the sun had climbed higher in the pale blue sky. Her son David had pulled in and was stocking the feed racks with hay and the troughs with ground grain.

"I think I'll go out and ask him what Ann is doing today. I need to get away for a while; separate my thoughts from the cloud of friction. Being with that daughter-in-law of mine is pure sunshine to my soul. If I call her she'll say she's free no matter how full her schedule is."

16

3/

Rachael walked slowly across the barn lot toward the board fence back of the hip-roofed barn. She noticed that the red paint was beginning to flake in places. It hadn't been painted since her husband died seven years before.

She saw a few Canadian thistles growing, getting a head start, along the fencerow. It would never do to let them go to seed. "I'll get out here and chop them off and burn them with the brush from the orchard."

She and her son had managed to keep up the buildings and grounds and fences. It had been important to John Brooks and they wanted to honor him by maintaining things as he left them.

Rachael often thought that Sam Clinton must be disappointed that the hundred and ten acres weren't going to rack and ruin. He'd wanted the place to go with his mother's seventy since he'd inherited the land down the road. He had tried to buy it from John once or twice, then knew when to take no for an answer. But he'd not quit pestering Rachael to sell. He wouldn't accept the fact that he was wasting his time.

Rachael leaned her arms on the slanting top board of the fence and watched her son fork hay into the slatted racks. His arms moved in a swinging rhythm. A surge of love flooded her mind, love for the tall gentle man who was her son. She remembered some of the times when she'd prayed for wisdom and asked for guidance in keeping his God-derived nature from being corrupted or scarred. Now as David walked toward her with his brown mesh work hat far back on his head she felt a welling sense of gratitude for answered prayers.

"Hi, Rachael Elizabeth," David Brooks said as he climbed the fence in two steps up and two down. "How's the world treating you today?"

"Good," Rachael said. "But some of the people in it are whittling my peace of mind a little."

"Who, for instance?"

"Oh, you know. The church fight seems to be getting worse."

"That's true, I've seen signs."

"Like what?" Rachael asked.

"Oh, what you'd expect," David said. "I was at the parsonage yesterday afternoon helping Ken unclog the drain to the kitchen sink. There was a regular parade. Women bringing food. First one side, then the other. That preacher's got enough pies, cookies, and nut bread to have his own bake sale."

"I suppose everyone tried to line him up on their side," Rachael said.

"Well. They probably had it in mind. But Ken didn't give anyone a chance. He brought them out to the kitchen. Naturally they wouldn't talk in front of me."

"Naturally. That's *one* advantage of having me for

your mother."

David grinned. "You don't have to fish for a compliment. You're a big plus in my life. We both know it — so does Ann."

"By the way that's what I came out to ask you. Does Ann have anything big planned for today?"

"I don't know for sure," David said. "She was on the phone when I left. Long distance. From someone in Newcastle. Why? What's on your mind?"

"Oh, I sort of have itchy feet. I thought maybe Ann and I could go shopping and eat out. Get away from the problems which buzz and zing in my mind."

"Then call her," David said. "I'm going to a sale over north of Parker. She won't have to cook for me."

"Oh, I hate to ask," Rachael said. "She'd drop anyting — " She looked up to see Ann's bronze compact car pulling in the gate.

"See, you don't have to call," David said. "I still say you gals have ESP going between you."

Ann Hayward Brooks had been a private secretary before her marriage to Rachael's son. Her slender figure and misty blue eyes had a kind of a Dresden figurine look, fragile, precious, and lovely. But her mind was precise, accurate, and logical. Rachael depended on her daughter-in-law. "She helps me think through problems," she'd often told Tilda. "Her clicking reasoning clears away some of the cobwebs. Another thing. She hasn't lived here long enough to have her thinking cluttered up by the prejudices and mixed-up opinions."

"I tried to call you," Ann said. "But you didn't answer. Want to go to Newcastle with me?"

David scratched his head. "You two! Mom was just

19

wishing you'd ask. Why you going?"

Ann smiled. "I'll tell you while Rachael gets ready. I'll go home, change, and be back in half an hour. OK?"

"OK. I'll let you two talk."

Within a few minutes Rachael was dressed in her new pink shantung shirtwaist dress. She'd made most of it but Ann had put the slash pockets in the blouse and tipped them with silk braid arrows.

As they headed toward Henry County, Ann told Rachael the reason for making the trip. "My Aunt Florence is starting a new venture. A gift shop in a way. Actually it's more of a local crafts shop. People are to bring in things like their needlework and pottery. Aunt Florence will sell them keeping a commission for herself."

Rachael's mind ran back to her conversation with Tilda. It was like when she set the needle of her phonograph back to hear a best-loved hymn again. The *How Great Thou Art* section of her Christmas record would be scratchy long before the other spaces.

"Oh, Ann, do you suppose people from outside the county could put things in your aunt's store?"

"Certainly. Why not? We'll ask her," Ann said. "I didn't get to tell you that's why I'm going. To set up some kind of bookkeeping method. But who do you have in mind?"

"Tilda," Rachael said. She described her friend's rugs and ropes of beads and told how she needed an interest as well as extra money.

"Sounds like they're made for each other," Ann said, "your friend's wares and my aunt's shop."

They stopped at a drive-in restaurant before going to the shop on Bunday Avenue. As they waited for their order Rachael said, "I love eating here. Some people turn up their noses at these places. But I think this one is great. Of course, I'm always liking what's not the thing, such as bakery cakes and wieners. You know those pictures in magazines where rooms are shown before and after being redecorated. Sometimes I like the before better than the after, and you're not supposed to."

Ann laughed. "Rachael Brooks! You're a rebel!"

"I know," Rachael said. "I think you're supposed to be. At least some times and against some things."

The work at the long narrow shop took nearly three hours. Ann worked over ledgers in the fenced-in office at the back. Rachael helped Florence Sawyer arrange the few consignments which had been delivered.

"This seems such a wonderful idea to me," Rachael said. "Some of these things are really lovely, like these organdy roses. Even the name sounds pretty."

"I know," Mrs. Sawyer said. "A young mother east of here makes those. She's quite clever and artistic."

"I guess I'm behind the times," Rachael said. "I didn't know such stores as these existed."

"They don't; not around here anyway. I got the idea when I visited my sister in Indianapolis last Christmas. But I'm like you. Creating is always good."

This remark led Rachael to mention Tilda's rugs and beads. Mrs. Sawyer said she'd be glad to put them on display. "Tell her to put the price on them and then I'll mark them up 10 percent."

Rachael smiled to herself as she set a family of rag dolls on a shelf. *I told Tilda to act on faith, but I didn't expect results so quickly.* She felt a sense of urgency. She wanted to take good news to her friend.

21

On the way home Ann talked about the dissension in the church. "I told Dave last night that I really feel sorry for Rev. Holden, especially for what he'll go through Sunday."

"Because it's his first sermon?" Rachael asked. "That is what you mean, isn't it?"

"Yes," Ann said. "Both sides will be listening to every word. They'll be looking for signs to see whether he's taking sides. They'll likely imagine he's saying things which he doesn't mean at all."

"I'm afraid you're right," Rachael said. "I've had the same thoughts. I even thought of warning Kenneth, telling him how important this first sermon could be. But you know me. I don't want even to *seem* to try to influence him."

"Have you seen him?" Ann asked. "Since that first day?"

"No. But I've wondered if he'd been able to dodge or ignore Lucy or Cora or their messengers."

"Probably not," Ann said. "Not unless he did as my grandpa used to threaten to do when Grandma nagged, crawl in a hole and pull the dirt in after him."

4/

Rachael bought six sugar-powdered cream puffs at the bakery in the shopping center on the west edge of Newcastle. She gave four to Ann. After her daughter-in-law drove on, Rachael hurried to feed her dozen hens and put food in Tramp's pan in front of the doghouse. She had a place to go.

She decided to drive up to Tilda's. "Walking's fine for daylight, but I might not get home before dark." For some reason she could not explain why she left the linen-shaded lamp burning and put a note on the door saying she'd be sure to be back before nine. It wasn't because she was afraid to come home to a darkened house. David would have called this urge to leave word of the time of her return one of her mystical messages.

Tilda was scrambling eggs in a small frying pan when Rachael tapped on the frame of the screen door. "Come in, neighbor," she said. "Did you eat yet?"

"No. Not yet," Rachael said.

"Then I'll break a couple more eggs, maybe even three. I was just thinking that one doesn't make much scrambled eggs. Not worth washing a skillet."

23

"I brought something for dessert," Rachael said. "But I can't wait to tell you my news. Why I came."

"Then pour us some lemonade and let's hear it," Tilda said.

As Rachael spoke, she could almost see new light and life flow into her friend. "I can't believe what I'm hearing," Tilda said now and then as she heard the details of what Florence Sawyer had said.

As realization came, hope and enthusiasm shone in her eyes and bubbled in her voice.

"I've got one rug more'n three-fourths done," she said. "It's a wreath of roses. I started another some time back, an American eagle. I'll drive in and cut more wool strips."

"You have plenty of discarded clothing?"

"A couple of bushels," Tilda said. "My niece in Portland saves things as well as a couple of her neighbors. The only color I'm short of is green. It takes more of that shade. All flowers have leaves."

"I have a white wool blanket that's too thread worn for warmth. Could you dye it?"

"I sure could."

Rachael insisted that her friend bring out her materials. "I'll stay a while and cut a few strips, if you'll show me how wide — or narrow."

The scissors whispered and rasped and the rug hook scratched through the coarse burlap backing for over an hour. Tilda said she had enough beads to finish up three necklaces. "Then I'll have to get into town and get more. Say — there's a hitch! How'm I going to get things down to Newcastle?"

"That's no problem," Rachael said. "Ann goes down every Thursday. She keeps books for the Haywards' family doctor."

"I always did say that the good Lord made neighbors like you," Tilda said.

Two grapefruit-sized balls of wool strips, one red and one lavender, were ready for hooking before Rachael left for home. The conversation had run easy, casual, and free of any disturbing thoughts.

Tilda was already beginning to plan. "The first thing I aim to do if this lady sells my stuff is fix the roof. *Then* the walls of these two back rooms are going to get a thick coat of paint. There are so many water stains on this wallpaper that a person can barely tell where the roses are — or were. I think I'll buy yellow paint. Like sunshine.

"I don't aim to dishonor Frank's memory. But through the years I sort of adjusted to his way of thinking. It was easier to accept his view that money spent on the house was a luxury than to want things pretty — like your house. Or to expect them."

Rachael hadn't realized that her friend even wanted to fix up her house. In fact, she'd fought thinking critical thoughts of Tilda, thinking she'd got to the point of not really caring how her place looked. She'd moved out of the square eight rooms of the old frame house and lived in the two rooms which shedded off the back. They'd grown shabbier in the last four years.

When anyone condemned Tilda for letting things run down, Rachael always stood up for her friend. She'd say that Tilda always did choose to use her time in other ways. Like helping her husband with the farming and working in her garden where the sticky clay soil hampered her efforts considerably.

But Frank Barley had been gone for six or seven years and it *was* hard to see what Tilda did with her time.

As Rachael brushed the wool lint from her skirt onto a newspaper, Tilda gave her a clue as to why she'd neglected to keep up her home. "It's like a tight band was off my chest," she said. "I been scared to spend any of Frank's insurance, thinking I might need it to take care of me. I reckon that's natural not having any close relatives."

"I suppose so," Rachael said. "But I think we all have something of the same feeling. Not wanting to be a burden to anyone."

"But now," Tilda said, "all kinds of ideas keep popping into my head. But never fear! I'm not counting on every egg to hatch. Just a few."

Rachael drove slowly down the one street of Willow Bend. Two boys were playing basketball on the hard-packed patch of ground at the end of Jim Hart's garage. She caught glimpses of television screens in a few windows. Two showed colored pictures.

No light was on in the stucco parsonage unless it was in the study at the corner. It couldn't be seen from the road.

Sam Clinton's gray brick house was at the end of the street. Three cars were lined up on the only paved drive in the village. "I wonder who — " Rachael shook her head as if to rid it of speculation. "I'm not going to clutter my mind about who's at Sam's and why. Not tonight. It'd fog the brightness of the day." But she couldn't help seeing that Walter Landess' new station wagon was at the end of the line.

26

Rachael was tired but not sleepy. She looked in the back bedroom closet which David called Mom's Bin of Indecision. It held things she didn't use, and probably never would, but couldn't bear to throw away. She slid hangers along the broomstick pole and took two garments from the shoulder-shaped wires. One was bittersweet colored, a skirt which was still perfectly good, except for a patch of moth holes at the waistband. The other was a pale gray jacket she'd made years ago. It never did fit right at the armholes. It might be good background for Tilda's rug.

She took the wool, her scissors, and a small cardboard box to her rose armchair, and moved the lamp closer to her elbow. She looked around the room, seeing it not only as a familiar place but also through Tilda's eyes. *It is pleasant.* Her eyes moved from the bookcases to the fruitwood desk and the soft tan couch. She saw little things, the velvet pillows, brass stamp box, and the three-legged candy dish. This fluted China dish which was sprigged with pencil-point rosebuds had been her grandmother's. Her son David had sold packets of garden seeds up and down the Macedonia Pike, saved the premiums, and used them to send for the small rose-shaded lamp on the desk. A room of memories, of symbols of love, and a place where the nature of the inhabitant was in harmony with the evidence of her taste, choices, and treasures.

She'd worked for nearly half an hour when she saw the sweep of lights, made by a car pulling in the barn lot gate. Rachael glanced at the clock. *Five until nine. Who'd be coming now?*

She saw the shadow of a tall figure moving toward

the back gate. As it entered the circle of light cast by the pole lantern in the yard she recognized the young minister.

She met him at the door and saw at once that he was troubled. His gray eyes were clouded and there was even a line of white around his mouth. A sign of strain? Or anger?

"Come in and sit down," Rachael said. "Something's wrong. So don't bother to pretend. Tell if it'll help."

Kenneth Holden sat down on the end of the couch and shook his head. "I don't know where to begin. Or maybe I should be more honest. Actually I've been thinking of ending, not beginning."

Rachael bit her underlip while she sorted the intuitive thoughts which were flooding her mind. Someone had made a bold move to influence the minister, or even to dictate to him. It made little difference which faction had sent an emissary. Or had he been contacted by both?

"Do you mean you're thinking about resigning?" she asked.

A flicker of a grin moved on his lips but no light shone in his eyes. "Wouldn't that be something! Giving up before I've even preached one sermon. And on my first assignment. That would certainly be a black mark on my record."

"Yes, it would. But you didn't answer. Is that what you meant?"

"I thought of it," Ken said. "But I won't give up that soon. I couldn't. A half hour ago I was calling myself a fool for being bound and determined to stay."

"You had a visitor."

"A committee of visitors," Ken said. "A formidable

28

lineup of pillars of the church. Chairman of the board of stewards."

"Sam Clinton," Rachael said.

"And assistant superintendent of the Sunday school," Ken said.

"Loring Burke. He's Sam's brother-in-law."

"That figures," Ken said. "And there was one more. The head of the board of missions."

"That's Cora," Rachael said. "You don't have to tell me why they came. To tell you who's who and what's what." She smiled. "That's Sam's way of saying that the people who pay the most money ought to have the most say-so. Not the newcomers who'll like as not move on any day. No roots."

The minister took off his glasses and tapped them on his knee. "Sounds as though you were there," he said. "You quoted Mr. Clinton exactly."

"That's not surprising. I've been hearing that speech off and on for years. Sam's not given to originality and variety. He's lined up any number of preachers and township officials with that kind of yardstick."

"Does everyone go along with him?"

"Not everyone," Rachael said. "Not quite."

Neither spoke for several minutes. The faint click of the ticking clock measured the time of silence. The evening breeze rustled the wisteria vine on the side of the house.

"They came to line you up before you preached your first sermon," Rachael said. "Did they tell you what to say?"

"No. Not in so many words," Ken said. "But I had the feeling they had one picked out. Or maybe even two or three."

"Had you already decided?" Rachael asked.

"Yes, indeed," Ken said. "I wouldn't leave *this* to the last minute. I've polished and burnished every sentence. And replaced some of my gems of wisdom with others. Do you want to know the subject?"

"No," Rachael said. "I'll wait. *And* trust."

The young man smiled and the line of strain was gone. "That's what I came to hear," he said. "A trusting word."

5/

The rumble of thunder came from the west and woke Rachael the next morning. Within a few minutes the first raindrops pelted on the tin roof of the back porch. By the time she'd closed the west windows the pelting had increased to a bouncy drumming.

There'd be no plowing today. Farmers would congregate in places like Sam Clinton's garage or in barns. They'd talk about many subjects and against things like the weather, the government, and the proposed school addition. The people who were for things rarely felt the need to reinforce their feelings by rehearsing them to the like-minded. *No doubt the new preacher's name will be a topic of talk.*

A wet and dripping day had good and bad points. It was restful for one thing. The sight of rain streaming down the windowpane or making thousands of shining windows on the mesh of the screenwire seemed soothing. But Rachael only had so many rainy day jobs now. As she brushed and braided her hair she thought, "Am I in the same fix as Tilda? Do I need to find a new interest

— widen my horizons — just a little anyway?"

As the water in the copper teakettle came to a whistling boil Rachael put in a long-distance call to her sister-in-law in Dalton. When Dana answered, Rachael said, "Nothing's wrong. I just took a notion to call. I was wondering. Could you and Bob come over and eat with me tomorrow?"

"Oh, Rachael, I'd love to," Dana said. "It's been two or three months of Sundays since we had time for a visit. But it'd have to be a late meal. Bob is assistant superintendent at Sunday school and the regular one's going someplace. It would be one to two o'clock before we could get there. Would that put you out?"

"Certainly not. I'll plan on seeing you. Tell Bob I'll see if Ann and David are free. So he won't feel so outnumbered."

The prospect of having company gave direction to the day. *If there's anything I'm real good at it's organizing a meal. There's a kind of rhythm — a knowing what to do next. Is there anyone or anyplace for such a knack?*

She cleaned the house and put clean paper in the silverware and utensil drawers. As she swept, polished, and scrubbed she planned the next day's meal. *I'll kill a hen. That'll be a treat for Bob. He's partial to my baked dumplings.* She thought of the asparagus in the crisper drawer. *Maybe by tomorrow there'll be enough for at least a taste for all of us.*

She was chopping rhubarb into inch-long pieces when someone rapped at the back door. As she crossed the kitchen she caught of glimpse of herself in the round mirror. *Flour on my cheek as usual. I'm a dusty baker.*

Lucy Cavanaugh was standing on the step. Rachael

32

couldn't have been more surprised to see anyone — unless it was Cora Landess.

"Well — hello, Lucy — "

"Could I talk to you a while, Rachael?" Lucy asked.

Rachael was filled with quick impressions. It was as though a projector was showing slides in rapid succession. Click. Flash. Flutter. She wished she could say she was leaving on some important errand. *But I'm not. Not with flour on my face and a paring knife in my hand.*

"Well — of course," she said. "Come on in."

"I can see you're busy," Lucy said. "I'll just sit here in the kitchen."

Lucy's voice was shrill and strained. She seemed to be speaking through a clogged filter of great anxiety. Rachael was familiar with that tone of voice. She'd heard it in her own speech during the months of her husband's final illness.

"You can sit there in the rocker until I get these pies in the oven," Rachael said. "I won't take more'n two shakes."

She filled the dough-lined pans with fruit, sprinkled them with sugar, and dusted flour over the top. As she tucked the top crust over the edges she glanced at Lucy. She was sitting almost on the edge of the chair, working her fingers back and forth on the curved end of the arm.

Rachael had known Lucy for almost as long as she'd been friends with Tilda Barley, but they'd rarely visited in each other's homes. They'd worked together at church, in the women's circle, and sometimes on Red Cross and community fund drives. But Lucy was as much of a socialite as the neighborhood allowed. She gave much more of her time and energy to district church offices than to local responsibility. In fact, some of the circle members felt the Willow Bend congregation was nothing more than a stepping-stone for Lucy's high-toned ambitions. Rachael always felt that Cora Landess had coined this criticism. Cora and Lucy had been antagonists for a long time.

Lately Rachael had tried to remember when the enmity sprouted. There had to be a reason. There always is.

As she worked, Lucy began to talk in a few jerky sentences. "The rain seems to be letting up. I skidded in the soft gravel up the road. I didn't mean to track in."

Rachael slid the pies on the top rack and washed her hands. "Now, come in the living room and tell me what's on your mind." At the door she added. "But I have to tell you, Lucy, I don't want to hear about the trouble or be pressured to take sides. Here, sit in this chair."

Lucy fingered the amber clasp of her square alligator purse. Then she leaned her head back and began to talk. "I know better than to try to hash the whole thing over with you," she said. "I'm bone tired of the whole mess myself." Tears began to roll down her cheeks. No sobs. Just tears. But they seemed to relieve the strain in Lucy's voice. "I'm at the point now where I'd like to resign from everything, my church and circle offices. Maybe even from this neighborhood. I'd just like to move out."

"But that's not really what you mean, is it, Lucy? You know you love your home. And you've made so many improvements."

"I know," Lucy said. "And you're right. It's this

bitter feud I'd like to run away and leave."

"Then why don't you?" Rachael said. "Just drop out of the battle — desert, go AWOL."

"It's not that simple," Lucy said. "This rift began with Cora and me. And I did some recruiting. I admit that. And for a long time I enjoyed the excitement. Isn't that terrible!"

"Yes, it is," Rachael said. "Terrible but not uncommon."

"But it's gone too far and the way it looks to me no one's going to win."

"That's true of many conflicts," Rachael said.

"The church attendance is way down," Lucy said. "And a lot of us that still go do so for the wrong reasons. To keep the other side from getting the upper hand."

"But I still don't understand why you can't drop the whole thing," Rachael said. "Could you go to Cora?"

"What do you think!" Lucy asked. "Would Cora listen?"

Rachael shook her head. "No. I'm afraid not. But what if you'd refuse to take park in the fussing?"

"I'm trying," Lucy said. "But so many people are involved now. They keep calling me on the phone and dropping in. They've heard some juicy news or have some idea for getting ahead of Cora."

"Like influencing the new minister?" Rachael asked.

"Yes. I should have known you'd see that," Lucy said. "But I've drawn the line there — but others haven't."

Before Lucy left Rachael asked her what had brought her to the point of regretting that she was a part of the conflict. The answer was that in the first place she was weary, that her mind was tormented by all the hate and jealousy.

"But the clinching moment came when I got a letter from our Larry, from seminary," Lucy said. "I'd kept the news from him — about the rift in the church. He's not been here much as you know. I'd written that we were getting a new minister, one who was not out of school. Two sentences were like a call for retreat. He said, 'It must be rough going into a new community. I'll soon know, won't I, Mother?' "

"Oh, Rachael," Lucy said. "That hurt. I pictured Larry taking a pastorate like Willow Bend. One where two feuding women had led the congregation to take sides in a kind of civil war."

"I see, and I understand," Rachael said.

"This is why I came," Lucy said. "How *do* you stay out of fights?"

"It's not always as easy as this is going to sound. I simply refuse to listen to either side."

"That stops them from bothering you?"

"Maybe not at first," Rachael said. "But they soon give up."

"Do you think *I* could do it?" Lucy asked.

"You can. But you'll have to be firm and consistent. Don't talk to *anyone* on either side."

"You can't mean you *never* talk about what's going on," Lucy said.

"Only with other neutrals. Like Ann and Tilda and David."

"That doesn't leave many — if you only can discuss the fight with those who aren't on one side or the other."

"I'm not so sure about that. There are some — a few — who are what David calls 'smilingly mum.' They keep on going, keep on nodding and waving, but not saying what they think."

"But I don't think they're what the newscasters call the silent majority."

"No," Rachael admitted. "But sometimes a minority gets things done. Look at the disciples."

6/

The rain stopped a little before sunset. The gray blue clouds of early evening were underlined with streaks of orange. The setting sun shining through this layer of color cast a greenish bronze light over the world.

Rachael walked slowly through the yard looking for the effects of the daylong drizzle. The tight purple buds of the lilac were opening into lavender stars and the spires of the iris leaves had grown at least an inch. It was a time of flowering.

The world seemed lovely — and a little hushed — or was it waiting? And for what?

David and Ann came by as Rachael walked up the back steps. "We're going in to the shopping center," her son called. "Want to hitch a ride?"

"Well, I might as well, I guess," Rachael said. "I don't need much. But I did think it might be nice to have a spring salad tomorrow, and I'm fresh out of head lettuce."

"Well grab your purse or whatever," Ann said.

The trip took up a large chunk of the evening. There was enough time for Rachael to study her Sunday school lesson and mix the dough for her icebox yeast rolls before her eyelids began to feel heavy. She felt as though she had to prop them up to see the last quarter hour of her favorite television musical.

She awoke to the liquid twittering of the nesting sparrows in the tangle of honeysuckle vines which clung to the back of the house. This particular sound reminded her of the bird-shaped tin whistles that were sold at the county fairs and at stands in front of the circus tent on Macedonia Avenue. A tablespoon or two of water in the open bowl made the same gargling tweet. Or which resembled which?

The sun came up on a clean and lovely world. Perfection seemed to be depicted in the flowers, the graceful branching of the trees, and in the thick carpet of grass. *It's only our thinking that's out of harmony.*

Rachael preferred to walk to church when the weather was fair. By now this fact was generally known. Passersby might not understand why anyone chose to wear out shoe leather when they might ride. But they'd learned that she really meant it when she said she enjoyed walking.

She was more certain about wanting to be alone this morning. She always felt as though she should move to church in a prayerful attitude, but this feeling was even stronger than usual. She could have ridden with her son and his wife and been quiet but they were going to Ann's home church in Newcastle. Ann's brother was to be the lay speaker.

"And I could have driven," Rachael thought as she set her pink flower-encrusted hat over her braids. David called this process putting a pillbox over a doughnut. *If I don't drive the car more often I'll have to get the battery charged again.*

She stopped on the Cabin Creek bridge and watched the water tumble over the moss-covered rocks on its way to White River. The rippling was soothing music. Then she came to Sam Clinton's half-plowed field which sloped up from the creek bank. The furrow at the edge of the plowed part was banked with a high ridge. The sharp point of the share had rolled the sod into a long hump across the field.

Rachael stopped for a minute. Something had caught her attention. Rivulets of water were draining down from the high land. They were cutting into the ridged barrier, wearing it away in places.

As Rachael walked down the street of Willow Bend she tried to coax a Bible verse to become clearer in her mind. It kept floating at the edge of realization. *It's something about furrows. I'll have to look it up.*

In spite of her leisurely gait Rachael was one of the first to reach church. Rev. Holden was in the vestibule to greet the arrivals. He smiled and said, "Good morning, Mrs. Brooks."

Rachael peered inside, trying to get her eyes adjusted to the muted light. She saw three people standing within earshot, so she kept her greeting casual. "It *is* a good morning, isn't it?"

Cora Landess and Mr. and Mrs. Sam Clinton were watching her as she walked toward them. *Trying to read my mind.* She spoke and they nodded. And the four of them branched off to their usual seats.

Sam never sat with his wife, in church or much of anywhere else. He strode down the side aisle, across the front of the side of the pews to the right and sat down, turned a little sideways at the end of the second pew. From that place and position he could see all over the church. Who sat by who. What part of the sermon prompted one person to whisper to another, and whose children were acting up.

Rachael had known Sam as long as anyone in the township and that was as far back as she could recall. She remembered him as a boy, unsmiling, plodding, and given to violent rages when he was crossed. He hadn't changed. He was still stern and hardworking. But he'd changed his reaction to opposition. He no longer threw other boys' balls in the tall alfalfa or squashed green tomato worms in his opponent's books. He fought in other ways; ran someone against them in local elections, pestered them to buy their land, or blocked any move they made in church.

Tilda Barley came in to sit with Rachael and within ten minutes the bell began to clang. Connie James hurried down the side and arranged her music on the mahogany piano while the echoes died away.

The new minister walked down the aisle and stood behind the lectern. His glasses glinted in the light from the brass reading light.

"I've met some of you and the others have probably assumed that I'm the new minister. My name is Kenneth Holden. I grew up in a suburb of Detroit. I'm still in seminary and I'm unmarried. That's enough about me now."

The tall young man looked over the congregation. Then he began to rub a doubled fist up and down the slanted top of the lectern. "I understand that it is your custom

41

to have worship services before Sunday school. This may or may not be best for the effectiveness of the church. However, the policy will not be changed unless it is so decided by the official board."

"Oh! Oh!" Tilda whispered. "He'll run into trouble *there*. Walt Landess always heads for his fishing spot on the reservoir before the benediction's finished."

Rachael smiled. Tilda was right. The Landess children were grown and Walt wasn't the kind to care whether or not others would bring theirs to Sunday school more regularly if it were held at an earlier hour. This, as Tilda once said, was "no weightier than a mosquito leg to Walter."

Rachael felt sorry for Sue Hart, the songleader. For months she'd tried to lead people into singing in unison. But it seemed they couldn't put their hearts into songs like *Blest Be the Tie That Binds* and *Have Thine Own Way, Lord*. The binding tie was frayed and so many people had their minds set on bending others to their will, not on yielding to God's power.

A wave of discouragement swept over Rachael. Or was it despair. She shut the hymnal and listened to the lagging, spiritless singing. Would Willow Bend ever recover from this factional wound? Or would it be like Old Bethel Church over west, have the doors padlocked and finally be torn down? What could Rev. Holden say in this, or any number of sermons to break down the ridge of dissension?

The minister turned off the reading lamp, clasped his hands on the open Bible and began to talk — without notes. "I'm going to base this sermon on the twenty-sixth verse of the forty-fourth chapter of the Book of

42

Psalms. 'Arise for our help, and redeem us for thy mercies' sake." He paused, as if waiting for the words to soak in. The sentence, "My doctrine droppeth as the gentle rain," flitted into Rachael's mind.

The minister repeated his text, then he discussed several definitions of the word redeem. To make amends, to recover something lost, and release and restoration from bondage or captivity.

Someone cleared his throat. A few shiftings of feet could be heard from different areas of the church.

The minister went on to tell of the action of redemptive groups in other times and places. "The group which should be our model is the Twelve — the disciples. One was a traitor, others were fearful, or vacillating, or doubtful. But they, for the most part — were united for a common work — to carry the gospel of Christ to the waiting world."

Rachael felt as though she were hearing a clear call. The direct delivery, the pertinent sentences, and the spiritual challenge were so fitting. Would people listen? Could the message be put into practice?

After the last hymn, and before the benediction, the minister spoke again.

"I'm taking the inititative in starting what I hope will be a truly redeeming group. We will meet in the parsonage. I'm setting up the living room as a chapel.

"Anyone who is interested, no, I mean concerned, please be there at 7:30 on Monday evenings."

Rachael was wondering how these sessions would differ from the Wednesday night prayer meetings. They'd been little more than armed camps lately. Then the minister answered her questioning thoughts.

"These sessions will end with a prayer circle. The chairs will be so arranged that we can join hands as we invoke the blessing of God on our neighbor, our church, and our community."

"Oh! Oh," Tilda whispered. "It's likely to be a pretty small circle. A Lucy won't run the risk of having to sit next to a Cora."

7/

Rachael invited Kenneth Holden to eat Sunday dinner at her home. This was an impulsive act. She'd watched people file out of the church. Some shook hands with the minister. Some sneaked out the back door to avoid doing so. Some looked at him and smiled, others ducked their heads and sidled past.

There were a few who were visibly moved. Tilda patted the young man's arm and Connie James smiled through tears. Rachael waited until he was alone in the cube of a vestibule. Then she walked toward him.

Kenneth turned and his gray eyes asked the question. Her answer, "I was right to trust you."

"You think so?"

"Yes," Rachael said. "I have the feeling that if this approach doesn't help we're beyond redemption."

The rest of Sunday was pleasant. Ken and Rachael's brother walked into an immediate acquaintance. They discovered common interests such as baseball, history, and rock hunting. After the dishes were washed Bob took them for a drive. They went to Muncie and saw the university campus. Then they drove south to the rolling land of Henry County. Ken noticed that the name Raintree had been given to roads and restaurants. "That's because of the book *Raintree County*," Bob said. "It's supposed to be about this area." He went on to describe the lovely tree which showered sprays of yellow blossoms in the springtime, golden rain.

They'd reached Rachael's home a little before six and Kenneth said he needed to go back to the parsonage and study. "And write a letter to my aunt — the one who brought me up." Rachael gave him two cold chicken sandwiches and a sack of the rolled oats cookies.

Ken smiled as he took the package. "I'll tell you a secret," he said. "I was deluged with baked goods a few days ago. It wouldn't keep, so I hunted up the mission in town. Now I'm down to three brownies and a fourth of a loaf of nut bread."

The house seemed unusually quiet after the company left. She remembered feeling the same emptiness as a child. It seemed that the special activities of Sunday weren't enough to cover the whole day. A lonely and sad feeling came with evening. She recalled the turning (almost desperately) to homework or reading, as though this activity were a bridge to the usual, to purposeful activity.

She took the linen tablecloth off the drop leaf table and folded it carefully. The silky fern design was as beautiful as it had been when she hemmed the damask by hand fifteen — or was it sixteen — years ago?

When there was nothing else to put in order, Rachael decided to go up the Macedonia Pike to see Ann and David. She had another reason for going besides filling the void. They should know about the plan for

46

making a redemptive move.

David farmed the land east of his mother's farm. It ran from the east edge of the Brooks farm up to the corner where a narrow gravel road came to the paved Macedonia Pike. The rented farm had a six-room bungalow-type house where the owners had lived until they retired and moved to Florida.

It was a well-built house and in good repair. During the years since Ann came to live in it her taste and personality had gradually made imprints on the place. The colors of wall paint had been changed from harsh blue and garish green to shell pink and ivory beige. The dark walnut stain had been removed from the woodwork so that the satiny oak showed.

Ann met Rachael at the door and said, "Come in! It's been too long."

"Well," Rachael said, "you know me! I don't want to be an interfering mother-in-law."

"I know. But you bend so *far* backward," Ann said. "Dave's at the barn. Would you come out to the back porch? I sowed verbena seed in berry boxes and I don't know whether they're big enough to transplant."

Rachael inspected the fragile seedlings. "I think they are. Especially since the ground's so nice and moist. Why don't we do it — now."

"I didn't mean to involve you," Ann said, "but your green thumb *might* be a boost."

As they spaded, raked, and patted mealy soil around the threadlike roots Rachael told Ann about the morning services.

"That took courage," Ann said.

"I know," Rachael said. "Kenneth spoke quietly, yet

47

forcefully. I had the feeling that no one could help but know that he was fully aware of the dissension."

"I wonder," Ann said, "how many will come? Besides us."

"It's hard to say," Rachael answered. "Tilda said it'd be a small circle."

Rachael used much time in reading and studying during the next twenty-four hours. She looked up all the references to redeem, redemption, and redeemer in the concordance of the Bible and in the dictionary. She copied the text of the minister's sermon and meditated on its meaning. In a real way she felt as though she were preparing her mind for the meeting in the parsonage.

A mellow sunshine dried the rain-soaked soil in time for Rachael to set out the verbenas Ann had shared. Her land along the creek bed held water longer than other places. She ate an early supper of chopped head lettuce and creamed leftover chicken on toast. The phone rang as she racked her dishes.

"Rachael," Tilda Barley said, "you're coming up to church, I reckon."

"Yes. I'm ready to dress now. Ann's coming past. Do you have a ride?"

"Well, no," Tilda said. "I didn't want to call and ask anyone outright if they're going. Anyways, I can walk. It's not that far."

"Well, just as you wish," Rachael said. "But if no one shows up from out your way I'm sure Ann won't let you walk home alone."

"It's hard to tell who we'll see," Tilda said. "But I'll be surprised if *any* men come."

Rachael watched Tilda's face when she walked in the

dusk-shadowed room. She blinked when she saw David Brooks sitting on one side of the minister and Connie James' husband on the other. Although a flower sent to Connie's mother had been the spark that ignited the flare of antagonism the young couple had managed to avoid taking sides. Rachael often observed that some people could live above pettiness. Or was it apart?

Tilda's wasn't the only face to show surprise when Lucy Cavanaugh rapped on the wooden frame of the screen door. Rachael hadn't told anyone of Lucy's visit.

"Is it all right if *I* come?" Lucy said. She seemed uneasy and rubbed the left side of her face with trembling fingers.

"It *certainly* is," Kenneth said. "It certainly *is.*"

He looked at his watch. "It's about time to begin," he said. He began arranging chairs in the center of the room, each about one foot from the other. After the eight people moved to the circle the minister began to talk. "I've had one experience as a participant in a redemptive group. This was in Detroit, in a nondenominational community church." He took off his glasses and looked toward the window, as if peering into the past. "I'm sure the change which came to that congregation influenced me to study for the ministry. The spiritual effect of a redemptive group in rebuilding a splintered congregation made a deep and lasting impression on me."

He went on to outline his idea of what the meetings should include. "Now I'm not a dictator and any of you may have thoughts on this matter. But on one point I'll be firm — if not stubborn. The trouble in the church, or its cause, should never be mentioned. Agreed?"

The others nodded or echoed the word "Agreed."

49

"This is a time for prayer, either silent or audible. Or for Bible reading. I brought some Bibles from the church and gathered up mine. Does anyone here have any ideas on procedure? Or on hopes?"

"I was thinking this morning," Ann Brooks said. "It might unify our thinking if we picked out a text or topic to read and study the week before each meeting."

"Good," Kenneth said. "I'd had a similar idea. I meant to lead out with the text I used yesterday."

"We already seem to be thinking along the same lines," Rachael said. "I had that verse in my thinking a good part of the day."

"The prayer circle idea," Lucy said. "That appealed to me."

"We will have it at the close of every meeting. For a good reason," Kenneth said. "It's a moving and sort of tremulous experience. You may not want to talk for a while afterward."

The eight people discussed the text, asking questions, making comments, and interpreting meanings. The word "redeem" seemed to flower and assume significance.

Before the closing the minister spoke again. "There's another phase of this movement as it was carried out in my home church. That is that the trouble we're here to resolve should not be discussed by any of us with anyone. In a sense we turn a key to the door of that part of our minds. We open our hearts and thoughts to the influence of holy inspiration and guidance. Some people might warn you, at this point, not to expect miracles. I *do* expect them."

Then he collected the Bibles from which Tilda and Connie had read. He took his seat between Brad James and David. He talked softly and with reverence, telling of instances when Jesus met with His disciples and of His love for His followers.

"Now, let's form a circle with our hands. Shut our eyes. Think of the doctrine of Christ. . . . Now think of the persons you love most . . . picture them. . . . Now let that feeling go to the person on your right. Let it cover them. Then go on to the next . . . and the next."

The room was still. No cars passed. Not even a clock was within hearing distance.

"Now," the minister said. "Let this same warm feeling spread over the congregation. Omit *no one* whose face comes to your mind."

Lucy Cavanaugh's hand seemed to tighten on Rachael's.

The minister closed the session with the sentence, "Let the words of our mouths, and the meditations of our hearts, be acceptable in Thy sight, O Lord, our strength and our redeemer."

Rachael opened her eyes, blinked and took a deep breath. Everyone seemed to be doing the same.

The minister was right. This was not a time for talking. They seemed to be in a place apart. They smiled at each other, left the house, and walked down the chipped concrete steps. No one in the Brooks car said a word until David pulled in the barn lot gate.

8/

David turned the key
and the silencing of the motor allowed them to hear
the sounds of the summer night. The hoarse croaking
of frogs came from the banks of Cabin Creek. When their
pulsing, throaty, cry ebbed, the twittering sound of the
sparrows came from the wisteria vines.

"Some experience," David said, drawing a long breath.

"I know," Ann said. "If only everyone could feel as
we do right now. How will it work? This redemptive
action?"

"It's not for us to know that," Rachael said. "At least
not now. But I suppose it'll be because of the influence
of these meetings on us. And ours on others."

As she walked up to the back door the picture of the
ridged furrow in the field along the Macedonia Pike clicked
into her thought. *I didn't look for the Bible verse that
applies to this situation.*

She sat in the circle of light from the tall lamp and
leafed through the concordance. The verse she was hunting had something to do with ridges and water. But she
didn't find it in the references listed under these words.

Then she turned to the notations under furrows. And the first one adjusted her thoughts to assume a pattern. She dug into her purse for a small red-backed notebook and copied the tenth verse of the Sixty-fifth Psalm.

"Thou waterest the ridges thereof abundantly: thou settlest the furrows thereof: thou makest it soft with showers: thou blessest the springing thereof."

The phrases comforted Rachael's mind. The symbolism was meaningful and enlightening. Hadn't she just seen the effect of softening showers as she had many times before in her life? She'd known that hard-packed clods of soil became mealy with moisture and had seen the trickling rivulets of water break down ridges in the field up the road from the Cabin Creek bridge.

A long-held belief in the power of God seemed to enlarge into a state of deeper faith. *Like a butterfly emerges from the chrysalis or cocoon.* The possibility of a renewed fellowship began to flit into Rachael's thought at that moment.

She saw no one, in the Willow Bend congregation, other than Ann and David until late the next day, and for a good reason. She was at home only a few hours. Ken Holden's remark about taking baked goods to the mission in Muncie had aroused a flicker of interest.

She'd known that such a place existed, but that's about all. She had no idea how the venture was supported, or what it involved.

The idea of investigating the mission's purpose flowered as she washed the breakfast dishes on Tuesday morning. "It won't hurt to go in and see what goes on," she thought as she ran the dust mop over the kitchen floor.

She stopped at Tilda's to see if she needed anything from the city. She'd spoken of her short supply of oat beads. But her friend wasn't at home.

Rachael rapped on the door and walked around the corner of the house so that she could see the garden. Then she remembered. Tilda always left a note under the concrete urn on the side porch. "No need to let the whole wide world know my whereabouts. But there are a few who care. Like you."

The spicy fragrance of pink and white geraniums engulfed Rachael as she slid the scrap of lined paper from under the chipping urn. "Gone to town. Back at noon." the note said.

"How'd she go?" Rachael wondered. Tilda had never learned to drive and had sold Frank's chocolate brown sedan three or four years ago.

She had no trouble finding the mission, knowing that it was on South Jefferson. She'd traveled this access to Muncie all of her life. Old Pet, her father's trotter, had pulled the rubber-tired carriage along the brick street. By the time she was riding in automobiles a layer of concrete had been poured over the bumpy brick underlay.

Now most of the residences had been torn down and replaced by business buildings. A few, like the square frame home which housed the mission, had been converted to other uses.

A lump seemed to stick in Rachael's throat as she rang the bell at the door of the screened-in porch. Tilda called such feelings nervous knots. *I've been in a rut too long. New places and moves seem scary.*

A voice called, "Come in," and she opened the screen to see a wheelchair at the inner doorway. A woman who was somewhere near to forty propelled herself out of the way. One leg was in a cast.

"You wanting to see somebody?"

"Yes," Rachael said. "But I'm not sure who. The person in charge, I guess."

"That's Missus Fleming," the woman said. "She's upstairs." She rolled back to a square table and picked up a handbell. After the echoes of three sharp shakes died away Rachael heard footsteps coming down.

A tall young-looking woman came within sight on the landing. Her pepper-and-salt hair was cut short and shaped to her head. The only soft touch was in a pouf of fluffy bangs and in her powder-blue eyes.

"This lady wants to see you about somethin'," the occupant of the wheelchair said.

"Well, thank you, Bertha," Mrs. Fleming said. Then she smiled at Rachael. "Won't you sit down? I do have a small office. But the linoleum's just been waxed."

"This is fine," Rachael said. "I don't even know for sure I should be taking up your time, but I was wondering if there's anything I could do to help. As a volunteer."

"There probably is," Mrs. Fleming said. "We are called on to fill all kinds of needs. Tell me a little about your background."

As Rachael talked Mrs. Fleming began to nod. Her bangs bounced on her high forehead.

"You hadn't finished three sentences," the director said, "before I knew you were the person we needed for our cooking class." She went on to say that some women who'd been sheltered by the mission were now back in their old homes or were making fresh starts in new ones. "But their homemaking knowledge is scanty," Mrs. Fleming said. "They do badly, can't seem to manage time or money or themselves. The main need is to prepare nourishing meals on low budgets."

"Well," Rachael said. "I've done *that*."

"I assumed so," Mrs. Fleming said. "Now I've outlined a procedure. There are four people who need this type of help. My idea is to have them come in one day a week and prepare the noon and evening meals under supervision."

"Would there be funds for food — for supplies?" Rachael asked.

"We'd use what we have and those who are in the mission would eat with those who do the cooking. How does that sound?"

"It's a good plan," Rachael said. "But don't you *have* a cook?"

Mrs. Fleming smiled and lowered her voice. "Yes, we have a cook. But she can't stand to have anyone in the kitchen while she's at work. So! We'd do this on her day off. Now, Mrs. Brooks, would you want to help us?"

Rachael's first impulse was to say she'd need time to think. That she'd want to discuss the matter with her son. But she knew that she was just being reluctant to change the pattern of her days. She was sure that Ann and David would tell her to do what she thought best.

She drew a deep breath and said, "Suppose we put me on a trial basis. Set the classes up for a certain length of time, a month or six weeks. Just to see how it works out."

"That's fine with me," Mrs. Fleming said. "The next thing to be done is set a date, then comes menu planning — so we can order supplies. Would Friday be too soon? Or is that a bad day for you to come?"

"No. One day's as good as another," Rachael said. "Friday might be good for those in the class. It could lead them to fix better meals over the weekend." Then she smiled. "Or is Sunday dinner a special time for them, like it still is for us?"

"For some it is," Mrs. Fleming said. "A very few."

They decided that Rachael needed time to plan her menu. "I'll call you Thursday morning to give the order."

She hadn't reached the city limits before doubts began to nag at her mind. Perhaps she should have given herself time to weigh the matter. What kind of people would come to the classes? Was there any use to try to change adults?

"But it's too late to back out now. I guess I can stand it for a few weeks."

Tilda was leaving her mailbox as Rachael rounded the curve in the Macedonia Pike. So she pulled in the drive and went up to the porch where her friend waited.

"You been gadding, I see," Tilda said.

"Yes. I went into town," Rachael said. "I stopped by on the way."

"Well! I was in Muncie too. Lucy Cavanaugh called. She said she was going in to get some wallpaper and wanted to know if I needed anything."

"Lucy?" Rachael said. "That not like her. Did she — "

"Did she talk about the fuss?" Tilda said. "No. Not one word. When I asked her to pick up some beads she said for me to get myself ready and go along and that she was running into the drugstore.

"That was nice of her," Rachael said. "How you getting along anyway? With your crafts, I mean."

"Fine. The rose wreath rug is done. The edges bound and everything. Three strands of beads are ready for the clasps. I'm calling Ann pretty soon."

Tilda went on to say that she'd cut pictures of four rug patterns out of a needlework catalog and pasted them on a cardboard. "I figured some folks might see them and I'd get an order or two.

"I bought my paint today," Tilda said. "Just acted on faith and let loose of enough cash to buy two gallons. It's a color called Pale Jasmine. A real pretty shade."

"Are you going to put it on?" Rachael asked.

"Well, as you know, I'm not much on climbing. So Connie James is going to do the out-of-reach places from the floor parts."

"Connie?" Rachael said in surprise.

"Yes. She offered. Well, in a way we worked out a deal. Connie feels penned up these days. She loves to paint and hates to patch. So! I'm going to stay with the children and her mother and help her catch up on her mending."

Rachael smiled. "Sounds like old times. Trading work. But let me tell you what *I've* been up to. You aren't the only one that's brave enough to try new tricks."

9

Before Rachael left for home she asked Tilda to "eat a bite" with her. "No," she said after a pause. "It won't be just a snack. You and I do too much of that. I'll fry us some potatoes and brown a couple of slices of ham and we'll sit down and eat a real meal."

Three more balls of colored wool were cut before Tilda went home. Ann and David dropped in and heard about the visit to the mission.

"Do you think I acted too quickly?" Rachael asked. She watched her son's face. There was no guile in him. What he thought was to be seen on his face. It had always been so. She suddenly remembered when her son was in the first grade. His gray eyes were clouded when he walked in from the bus. A white line of strain edged his nostrils.

She'd known something was wrong but debated about prying. It was better to wait for communication to start naturally. The little boy walked toward his room and then stopped in the doorway. "Mom. What does it mean not to believe in something?"

"Well," Rachael answered, "it usually means a person doesn't think something is right. Why?"

"That's what Russel George said about movies. That their church doesn't believe in them. We go. *Is* it wrong?" David asked.

Rachael prayed for wisdom and the right words.

"Let's see if I can explain it," she said. "For a minute let's think of God's laws as a beautiful tree outside a building with many windows."

"Like the schoolhouse?"

"Yes. Like the schoolhouse. Some of us see the tree from one window. Some from another. But it's the same tree."

"Oh," the child said. Then he smiled and added, "I'm hungry." The signs of strain were gone. Evidently he understood as the twenty-five-year-old David did now.

"I don't see anything wrong with trying it, Mom. How else would you ever find out if it was worthwhile?"

"I took an elective course on quantity cooking," Ann said. I have my text with recipes. It might help."

"That's a fine idea. I'll borrow it tomorrow," Rachael said.

The younger Brooks were making a quick trip to the shopping center for grass seed and asked Rachael and Tilda to ride along. In one way Rachael would have preferred to stay home. She'd been on the go all day. But she'd sort of adopted a policy of going when she was asked. Maybe when she was in the mood no one would come along.

They let Tilda off at home on the way back and Ann picked up the finished rug, beads, and sample poster.

Rachael had trouble getting to sleep that night. Her

thoughts were busy rethinking the past and anticipating the next day. She decided to get up and read a while. "To stop this business of trying to eat yesterday's and to-morrow's dinner today."

She was away from home several hours the next day, borrowing the cookbook, taking her sweeper over to the shop in Moreland for repairs, and stopping by the nursery for snapdragon plants.

The subject of the rift in the church was wheeled to the outside rim of her thoughts, away from the hub of her immediate concern.

She listed the items on her menu. Stewing chickens, half and half cream and eggs for dumplings, potatoes, cabbage for coleslaw, and cake mix for an easy dessert. The cooking class members might be scared to try the dumplings but nothing could be easier, and there was no way they could fail to turn out tender and puffy. *If they pay attention.*

The telephones in Willow Bend were from the same exchange as the mission in Muncie. So Rachael went to the village to call in her list of supplies. She needed a few things from the local store too.

She bought most of her groceries from Lottie and Art Springer. They were friends. "And besides that, the General Store's handy. People will miss it more than they think if it closes. Even if all they buy is a loaf of bread now and then, or a pound of sixpenny nails."

Lottie rose from the tall stool behind the wooden counter. Rachael wondered why she wasn't in her usual place, the rocker with the seat of woven binder twine. It sat in the corner behind the stacks of overalls and work socks. This chair and two short pews from the old church flanked the tall *Warm Morning* stove. Rachael always knew when Lottie was keeping store. The minute the front door opened, the chair rockers squeaked as Mrs. Springer threw her weight forward in getting up to wait on customers. Art never sat in the chair and rarely anywhere else. He was what John Brooks had called "briggly." He lived on the move.

"Afternoon, Rachael," Lottie said. "My, you look pretty! That dress new?"

"Fairly so," Rachael said. "I've only worn it a half dozen times."

"Anything I can help you with?" Lottie asked.

"Yes. My brown sugar bucket is empty and I squeezed the last drop out of the vanilla bottle day before yesterday."

"Things do have a way of running out," Lottie said. "Of course, if they didn't we'd be all the way out of business."

Rachael helped herself to a loaf of whole wheat bread and two cans of Vienna sausage as Lottie scooped the soft caramel colored sugar out of the bin. Once or twice voices seemed to rise above the radio but Rachael thought it was the announcer until she'd paid Lottie and was ready to leave.

Then Sam Clinton's voice rose above the afternoon hymn. His strident tones canceled the melody of *Whispering Hope*.

"Say, I been meaning to ask you. You aiming to go to the new preacher's hand-holdings?"

Loring Burke's voice answered Sam. "Now, you know my wife! She won't let me sit up there holding on to some other woman's hand." A snicker accented Loring's meaning as it did almost everything he said.

"They know I'm here," Rachael thought. "This is all a

62

show for my benefit. Sam didn't have to ask what Loring thought. He *told* him what to think. That's the price Loring paid for marrying into the Clinton money."

She felt her cheeks getting hot. Ridicule was the most vicious of all weapons to her. Its point was sharp and barbed.

She glanced at Lottie, who shook her head and pursed her lips. There was nothing that could or should be said now.

A strong urge to go back and talk to Tilda about what she'd been meant to overhear almost influenced Rachael to turn the car around. *But that's what we're not to do. Repeat what we hear. Spread dissension.*

Her thoughts were churning, and discouragement was mixed with dread. She'd lived in the community long enough to know. Mockery had dimmed enthusiasm and curbed the implementation of many good intentions. Sam Clinton knew that ridicule was a powerfully effective tool. He'd used it before.

Doubts continued to creep into Rachael's mind. Sam and Loring probably wouldn't depend on her to spread the deriding words. They'd send out other sparks. Sometimes she compared the influence of such talk to a grass fire on a dry August day. Little tongues of flames darted in every direction, leaving a trail of seared blackened places.

I just hope Ken Holden doesn't hear, she thought as she ran the sweeper over the living room rug. Friday's cleaning would have to be done on other days for a few weeks.

The minister was at the seminary up north on Wednesday and Thursday. Sometimes he didn't start back until

Friday. His car was old and the tires were thin. The last class ended at six and any trouble would leave him stranded in darkness on the four-lane highway.

David had talked to his mother about Ken's car. "I don't think it's going to hold together until he finishes school. The going will be harder when winter comes."

Rachael had thought at the time that she for one would be glad to loan her car to the minister. But she doubted if he'd be willing to use it without paying. And if he had enough money to pay a rental type fee he could make payments for one of his own.

As the day ended, a sense of perspective eased her mind. Not everyone paid much attention to Sam Clinton's talk. Some were like those who attended the prayer meeting. There was another factor in the situation. More and more people were getting weary of the trouble. There seemed to be an unvoiced feeling that the Coras and Lucys should move their scrap to some private arena, take it out of the church.

The evening air was so warm that Rachael sat in the porch swing for over an hour after dark. The mock orange bush was in full bloom and the sweet and fruity aroma filled the air. A few cars passed. Someone's dog howled at the moon, which was a pale gold in the deep blue sky.

The ringing of the telephone broke into her reveries. "Rachael?" Ann's voice said. "You weren't asleep — I hope?"

"Oh, no."

"Well, I wanted to come down and wondered if it was too late."

"Never," Rachael said. "Is anything wrong?"

Ann hesitated, as if she was choosing her words carefully. "Nothing's wrong *here*," she said. "But I do have some news. Something I think you should know. See you."

Within a few minutes Rachael heard that Lucy Cavanaugh was in the Henry County Hospital. Ann had taken her mother in to see a neighbor and caught a glimpse of Lucy as they walked toward the elevator.

"But why down there?" Rachael asked.

"To get away from everyone who's mad at her on both sides," Ann said. "That's what she said. Her ulcer's flared up so she went to another doctor."

"No wonder," Rachael said. "All this hate and vengeance."

"She said that her husband's folks and some of their friends had called her a traitor for going to the meeting. That's what brought on the physical trouble. Anyway that's how Lucy feels."

"That's too bad. But to be expected," Rachael said. "The faction that's fought the Clinton group for control doesn't want their standard-bearer to desert. One of them may have to lead out, be in the front line."

The incident at the store was on the tip of Rachael's tongue but she swallowed hard. "I'll go down and see Lucy on Saturday," she said. "I'm sure we can talk about pleasant things. Lucy's ready, and so am I."

"And I have the feeling that several people feel the same way," Ann said. "I'm hopeful."

"Good," Rachael said. "Say, what did your aunt think of Tilda's handiwork?"

"Oh, I meant to tell you. The rug and one pair of beads were sold before I left. Here's Mrs. Barley's money. If you see her before I do, tell her Aunt Florence

65

thinks the rugs will go as fast as she can make them."

Rachael smiled. "I'm going to go up there the first thing in the morning. Good news should be spread freely."

10/

By the evening of the second redemptive prayer session Rachael was sure that some kind of force was at work in the neighborhood. She felt it in her own life and saw evidences of new life in Tilda's experience. These were good effects. But she wasn't confident that the leaven of prayer would be able to lift the church above the counteraction of Sam Clinton's influence.

She'd had time to think of the incident in the general store. Sam and his brother-in-law couldn't have just happened to be there when she stopped in for brown sugar and vanilla. Not that time of day. Not this time of year. The ground was dry enough to work and tractors were running up and down the valleys and back and forth on the slopes. The wet spring had delayed plowing, cultivating, and planting.

No, Sam had to be bound and determined about something to be sitting in the store in the middle of a sunny afternoon. Or had he been sitting? One of his fields ran within ten yards of the back of the store lot. *He could have seen my car. Motioned to Loring, and slipped in the side door. I wouldn't put it past him.*

She could only surmise what Sam would do to keep control. She didn't have much time for thinking about the matter until Saturday. The cooking classes at the mission had taken up most of Friday. She'd been exhausted that evening but felt the work was worth the effort. Two of the young mothers were halfhearted about the project but the other two were eager to learn and to work. One marveled that one egg and a cup of cream could turn flour into puffy tender dumplings. "I always figured it was a real complicated thing to turn out a good meal. That's why we've eaten mostly hot dogs and egg sandwiches in the eleven months since Joe and I got married."

The intention to go to Newcastle to see Lucy Cavanaugh was weak when Saturday morning came. "I'm tired and have things to do here. Besides, I'm not sure Lucy would be glad to see me."

In spite of all the doubting she headed south soon after noon. She took her time, enjoying the loveliness of early summer. The sky was a dome of cornflower blue, dotted with cottony clouds. A green fringe of trees bordered the horizon. She'd often thought that an Indiana spring was a kind of resurrection and that summer was a promise fulfilled. The bare black branches of the redbud trees were first embroidered in delicate sprays of fuchsia, and then became a parasol of fan-shaped leaves. The iris leaves were first seen as slender spires and then topped with orchid-like blooms. And the tall locust trees were appliqued first in fernlike leaves, then in fragrant white clusters.

There were very few cars in the Tarvia-surfaced parking lot behind the hospital. Rachael was more than fifteen minutes ahead of visiting hours. A steel blue pigeon strutted across the spongy black pavement coo-ing softly. *It knows this is a Quiet Zone.*

She waited in the long lobby until a volunteer Gray Lady took her seat at the head of the corridor leading to the elevators. She began handing out passes to visitors saying over and over, "Only two to a room, at one time."

When Rachael was at the head of the line she said, "I came to see Mrs. Lucy Cavanaugh. Is someone already with her?"

The lady behind the small desk riffled through the cards in the file. "No," she said. "She has very little company. Her room number is 218."

Sadness tinged Rachael's thought as she rode up in the cage of the elevator. Sociable Lucy was so alone now. It must be harder for her than for most people.

She paused in the door. Lucy's back was toward her. Was she asleep? Evidently not. She raised one arm and she ruffled the hair at the back of her neck.

"Lucy?"

Mrs. Cavanaugh turned over slowly and blinked to adjust her eyes to the shade of the room. "Oh, Rachael, come in."

"Should I?" Rachael asked. "Ann said you didn't want anyone to know you were here."

"Well, yes. That's what I told her," Lucy said. "But I figured that she'd tell you and you might come. But that's all right. I've cleared the air with you. Or have I?"

"You have," Rachael said. "How are you?"

"I'm better, much better," Lucy said. "The doctor told Ray I could go home the middle of next week. *If* I keep quiet."

"Do you think you can?" Rachael asked.

"Yes. I really believe so. I was thinking this morning. Being away this long has probably broken the habit people had of calling me all the time."

"That happens," Rachael said. "Like footprints fill in when the ground's dusty."

"Or when it's muddy," Lucy said.

She paused then said, "I'm not going to ask you if anything's happened. I don't want to hear."

"Some of it you will," Rachael said. She told about the sales of Tilda's rugs and beads, and her plans for fixing up her house. Then she went on to relate her own venture.

"My goodness," Lucy said. "You two are really branching out. Didn't it take courage to go in and work with people like that?"

Rachael flinched, inwardly at least. She'd never liked labels on people. They weren't big enough to tell the whole story, and usually listed only the worst.

"Well, they're people. They've been in trouble. And may be again. But if there's a chance they'll take an upward step — it's worth trying to nudge or support them."

Lucy didn't say anything for a few minutes. "That's what redeeming is all about isn't it?"

"Do you know! I never thought of that," Rachael said. "I'd only looked for signs of recovering in the church — in who attended and if they were friendlier to each other. But it could go on anywhere."

"I guess so," Lucy said. "Yeast doesn't leaven just one part of the dough. Remember, Rachael, how little blistery bumps came up here and there before the whole loaf raised? Back when we baked our own bread."

"They still do," Rachael said.

As Rachael walked up the Macedonia Pike to church the next morning she wondered how many people would come. More or less? Or was it too soon to see any change? Probably so.

She tried to avoid counting noses or looking around to see who was or was not in their usual places. She forced herself to center her thought on the idea that when two or more were gathered together in His name there He would be also.

She watched the minister's face as he took his place in the pulpit. She hadn't seen him since the session on Monday evening. He *looked* composed and his voice showed no sign of strain as he made announcements of coming activities. The prayer group, the Women's Circle, and the church board were to meet within the next five days.

Rachael hadn't realized that the next Thursday was the third one of the month, the regular Women's Circle day. Or did she subconsciously want to forget? The antagonism had been so strong at these gatherings lately.

Her attention was riveted on Kenneth's words when he began to list those in the congregation who were ill or in sorrow. Would he mention Lucy? Did he, or anyone, even know that she was in the hospital?

Evidently not. At least she wasn't named.

"I'll tell him after church," Rachael thought.

After the benediction Rachael turned to greet people. She'd always been a sort of self-appointed welcoming committee. It bothered her that so many people didn't seem to realize how it felt to be a newcomer. *But how could they? Willow Bend has been their church all their lives.*

71

Connie James came toward her. "Mrs. Brooks, some of our neighbors came. I want you to meet them."

Rachael saw five new people standing at the end of the aisle. Two men, two women, and a tall boy, of high school age.

"There are the Carders and the Laines," Connie said. "And this is Tim Laine."

"I'm glad to meet you and hope you want to come back," Rachael said.

"Thank you," Mrs. Laine said. "I think we will. Your minister came to see us yesterday. He impressed us — favorably."

"I have the same feeling," Rachael said.

Connie found a chance to whisper. "Our prayer circle will be larger tomorrow night."

Rachael felt a rush of gratitude for the fact that people like Connie James were in the world — and in the Willow Bend Church. It was strange in a way. The controversy had started over a flower sent to Connie's mother but neither of them had been drawn into the eddy of anger.

There wasn't an opportunity for Rachael to speak to Kenneth alone. But as she shook hands with him the minister said, "Will it be all right with you if I come down sometime this evening? To use your encyclopedias? My term paper isn't quite long enough. I need to pad it with a few paragraphs."

"You're welcome," Rachael said. "I'll be there as far as I know now. And if not I'll leave a note."

Rachael rode home with Ann and David. Before she got out of the car her son said, "Have you heard what Sam's up to now? About his remonstrance?"

"Remonstrance?" Rachael said. "Against what — of course! Against the new classrooms, the addition to the school."

"Right," David said. "He had only eight days left to file when he started around the township. He and Loring and Walt Landess, of course."

Thursday. The day he was in the store. Waylaying customers.

"Do you think he'll get enough names to outnumber those on the petition?" Ann asked.

"Why don't you come in?" Rachael said. "Then you can tell me all about it while I fix us a bite to eat. Or do you have plans?"

"No plans," Ann said. "I'd like to stay. But give me time to run up home. I made a pineapple cheesecake. OK by you, Dave?"

"OK by me," David said.

11 /

After the noon meal Rachael, Ann, and David sat on the front porch. Yellow and white butterflies floated in the silvery air. The leaves of the cottonwood trees whispered in the slight breeze and the fragrance of lilacs came from the tall bush at the corner.

They discussed Sam Clinton's move to block raising taxes to build a needed addition to the township school. It was an old story which had been repeated several times during the past ten or twelve years. The city limits had edged southwest and more people had moved outside their boundaries. "It's true that folks want to get out of the high tax rate districts," David said. "But it's also a fact that they couldn't build out here unless someone sold them patches of land. At a good stiff price, too."

"Then the housing project added to the problem," Ann said. "Brought the school enrollment up several notches. Does this mean it's an economic problem?"

Rachael shook her head. "Not altogether. There's more involved than people's pocketbooks." She went on to say that there were those who weren't in favor of any change. They either shut their eyes to what was going on or violently opposed any altering. Her voice was tinged with sadness as she made another observation. "As wrong as it may seem, a few have a low opinion of city people." She'd known other bitter feuds such as when land was condemned for highways and reservoirs. "It's shortsightedness maybe," she said. "At least about the water supply. Trees have been cut and ground plowed, letting rain run off and away. City people didn't do that. It's a big and complicated problem. And anger and hate and even greed make it hard to solve."

"Do you think this is connected with the church quarrel?" Ann asked. "Sam's move, I mean."

"Sure it is," Dave said. "He's showing his powerful fist in one place in order to scare people in another. And it's worked in times past."

"Yes, it has," Rachael said. "The Clinton money has impressed and ruled opinions and elections. But I have the feeling that that time is fading."

"Why, Mom?" David asked. "What makes you feel that way?"

"Well — because of what we just mentioned — the changing of the community. The new people, those who really think, haven't heard who's important around here. They probably won't listen if anyone tries to tell them. Of course, he can stir things up worse. Confuse thinking. Delay action. Cause hurt feelings. But even Sam can't stop change any more than he can prevent the falling of the rain."

Ann and David left in the middle of the afternoon.

They were sponsors of the youth group and were taking the members to an area meeting in Madison County.

"Is the attendance down any?" Rachael asked.

"Not much," Ann said. "Once in a while Lori Landess sends word she can't come because her folks are taking her someplace. But generally speaking the fussing hasn't touched the kids. They don't seem to pay attention. But that's been true for a long time, hasn't it?"

Rachael made a quick trip up to Tilda's, taking the balls of wool strips and a bundle of surplus asparagus stalks.

Her friend met her at the door. "Come in," she said. The clean smell of freshly painted rooms brought Tilda's plans back to Rachael's mind. She had been so busy herself that she hadn't kept tabs on what others were doing.

She stood in the doorway and looked around the long living room. "It's like a different place," she said. "I wouldn't have believed paint would make this much change."

"I know," Mrs. Barley said. "I catch myself just standing and looking. Sort of drinking it all in."

"It makes your furniture show up better," Rachael said. "Your mother's dry sink and the ladder-back chairs have taken on a new look."

"True," Tilda said. "Of course, I gave them a boost with a smidgen of furniture polish and a lot of elbow grease."

The two women talked for an hour. Tilda showed the finished eagle rug and one with an autumn leaf design which was nearly half done. "This one was ordered. I have two more to do, another rose wreath and one over the clown pattern for a child. My fingers are itching to do one of those."

"Do you think you'll ever run out of material?" Rachael asked.

"Well, maybe. For a while now and then. But I'm considering doing one or two in rug yarn to see if they'll sell. Of course, the wool strips make for a more genuine old-time look. I suppose it'll work out one way or another."

"You got anything planned for tonight?" Tilda said as Rachael rose to leave.

"No, except that the minister is coming down to look up something in my encyclopedias. Why?"

"Well, I've got this bee buzzing in my bonnet," Tilda said. "I don't know whether to shoo it away, swat it, or let it light."

"What's on your mind?"

"It's like this," Tilda said. "I got to thinking about Connie James. She's been so good to help me. She even collected a couple bushels of wool clothing from her neighbors in Candlewood Hills. I was thinking of finding a way of calling to offer to stay with her mother if they wanted to go anyplace this evening."

"So! That's your bee," Rachael said. "Do you want me to call for you?"

"Yes. I do. No use beating around the bush. And you don't need to bother letting me know yes or no. I'll get myself ready."

"All right," Rachael said. "If Kenneth has come and gone by the time you'd be supposed to go I'd like to visit with Mrs. Endicott. Any objections?"

"None," Tilda said. "The more the merrier, my father always said. But to my way of thinking the merry depends on who the more are."

Rachael smiled to herself as she drove home. Tilda's thinking, values, and beliefs were expressed in a truly individual way. Just as seeds sprouted, grew, and produced according to their nature. The golden, transparent wafers of parsnip seeds never produced tapered orange carrots. The smooth pellets which grew into radishes could never send out the crinkled pale green leaves of lettuce.

Connie James was pleased that Tilda had sent the message. "We haven't been to Winchester to see Brad's father in weeks."

They arranged that if Kenneth left before six-thirty Rachael would call, saying she'd bring Mrs. Barley. "Otherwise one of us will run over to get her."

Rachael turned from the telephone to see the minister walk past the kitchen window.

"I didn't hear your car," she said as she opened the screen door.

"You couldn't have," Ken said. "I walked. I'm trying to preserve that old buggy from all the struggle possible."

"It *is* running then?" Rachael asked.

"Yes, thanks to Tim Laine."

"Tim, oh, he's the tall boy who was in church today."

"Yes. I met him Saturday afternoon when I was over in the Hills. He heard my car coughing and spluttering and offered to come over to see whether he could find the trouble. He's a marvel. In half an hour the motor was purring like a kitten — a slightly hoarse kitten. I guess they have a course in school — on auto repair."

"Yes. I know," Rachael said. "The teacher's trying hard to find room and tools. He says the vocational side of education is important. But you didn't come down here to talk to me. Go on in."

Kenneth worked for an hour and a half. He was so absorbed that Rachael wasn't sure he saw or heard her tiptoe in the room and put a tray at his elbow After he left she saw that the pimento cheese sandwiches and lemon chiffon pie were gone. A folded note lay on the tray. She picked it up and read. "Bless you for being the keeper of the light in my personal haven from storms."

She wondered how much he knew of what was going on. Then she remembered. *I didn't tell him about Lucy being in the hospital.*

She took time to stop at the parsonage on the way to pick up Tilda. Ken didn't hear her stop and was busy ironing a white shirt, using a folded towel on a table for the pressing board. Rachael shook her head. "You shouldn't have to do this for yourself. You need mothering." She wouldn't leave until he gathered up all that needed laundering. "Just count this as part of my donation," she said. "I don't have enough to keep my automatic washer from getting rusty."

Ken smiled and shook his head. "You certainly have a way of making a person feel better, Mrs. B."

"Things bothering you tonight?"

"No. Not really. I feel more hopeful but I can't say why."

This gave Rachael an opening to tell about Lucy's visit to her and her present illness.

Later, Tilda saw the bundle of clothes on the back seat of the car. "Taking in washing?"

"No. Just doing what I see to do — they're Kenneth's."

"Oh, I see."

The visit in Candlewood Hills lasted much later than Rachael had expected. After Connie and Brad returned, the five grownups talked in the screened porch. Mrs. Endicott's wheelchair allowed her to join the others. The conversation was casual until Tilda said, "We've all been blind as bats in broad daylight."

The others looked puzzled and even a little shocked.

"Oh," Tilda said. "I'm as bad as the rest of you.'"

"Tilda — explain yourself," Rachael said.

"It's plain as the nose on your face. Of course you have to look in a mirror to see it. That's what I just did. Took a good look at myself. Here we are thinking about what that young preacher can do for us; asking ourselves how long it's going to take him to settle a fuss he didn't cause. How about him? A young man living alone, on a shirttail salary and spending big chunks of it to keep that car running so he can finish his schooling. What do we do? Nothing as far as I know — until Rachael picked up his laundry this evening."

Brad James drew a deep breath and pounded one fist into the palm of the other hand. "She's right," he said. "One hundred percent right."

They talked for half an hour. But it was Mrs. Endicott who brought the conversation to a purposeful focus.

"I'm more of an outsider than anyone here," she said softly. "But sometimes that's good. My husband used to say that anyone who stood one foot from an elephant couldn't describe the whole of it. But as you talked, this thought came to me. Why not another redemptive movement, one within a larger circle. A personal secretly operated activity."

"To support Ken. That's what you mean, isn't it, Mother?" Connie asked.

"Yes. You couldn't make such a resolution in his presence."

"But *we* can, the five of us," Rachael said. "Look for ways to support and encourage Kenneth."

"That's the ticket!" Tilda said. "I didn't know what was called for. Just that something needed doing."

"There are others who'd honestly like to help," Brad said. "Tom Laine was asking me today how Ken's car ever made those long trips every week."

"This wouldn't be the kind of activity that would take a group meeting, would it?" Rachael asked. "Just person to person communicating."

"I'd think so," Connie said. "None of us will be careless who we contact. We'd not want Ken's pride to be hurt. The news of private meetings might puzzle him."

"But it'll take prayer. Personal ones," Tilda said. "A lot of asking and listening so we can see ways of helping."

The two friends rode back toward Willow Bend without saying much. Rachael felt a sense of hope and even of wonder. The Spirit of the Lord was a real presence.

12/

Rachael slept later than usual the next morning. The chuffing chug of a tractor brought her to awareness. "That's David," she thought. "He's going to plant the back field today."

She moved with a more lively pace for the next two hours. There'd be someone besides herself to feed at noon. She took a package of round steak out of the freezer to thaw before she made toast and cooked oatmeal for her breakfast.

"I'll make a bread pudding. David loves it and I'm getting a surplus of bread crusts." She liked the way she worked that morning, with rhythm and precision. *Some days I'm all thumbs.*

She hurried out to the garden a little after ten o'clock to see if any of the winter onions were big enough to eat. She stood at the edge of the yard appreciating the lovely sights. The wheat field across the fence was a rippling sea of fresh green. A hawk soared and dipped above the Yellow Transparent apple tree. Could it smell the ripening fruit?

Then she heard the rumble of the loose planks on the

Cabin Creek bridge. As she started up the back step she saw Sam Clinton drive slowly past the house. *He's up to something or he'd be in the field.*

She nodded and didn't look to see if Sam spoke to her. She often said that this practice saved a lot of hurt feelings. *Besides, I'm not even sure Sam saw me.*

Within fifteen minutes Rachael faced the fact that she'd been seen. She was browning the floured pieces of steak when someone pounded, not rapped, not knocked, but pounded on the back screen door.

She turned the heat to simmer and turned to see Sam. Her heart thumped. *Talking to him's not my idea of a good way to spend a pleasant summer day.*

"How do, Rachael," Sam said.

"Good morning."

The stocky man backed down to the bottom step. Rachael stood inside the screen and looked at him through a fine black mesh.

"I come to give you a chance to sign this paper."

"You mean the petition against the addition to the school?"

"Yep. Us landowners gotta do something to keep from having high taxes eat us up," Sam said.

Rachael drew a deep breath. She thrust one hand into the pocket of her pink flowered dress and opened and closed her fingers to ease the strain. "Samuel Andrew Clinton! You know I won't sign that paper. Why did you even bother to stop here?"

Sam reached up and set the gray felt hat on the back of his head. The first time Rachael heard the phrase *status symbol* she thought of Sam's hat. He never wore denim or leather caps or straw hats like other farmers.

Winter and summer alike his headgear was a dented crown felt with a black grosgrain ribbon above the turned down brim.

Sometimes Sam used that brim to shade his eyes, or as Tilda once said "to hide his shiftiness." Now the hat was out of the way. Rachael could see the anger in Sam's steel-blue eyes.

"I don't understand your way of thinking."

"Well, that's not new," Rachael said. "You never did."

Sam's ruddy face deepened to a purplish shade. He'd never seen why a girl called Rachael Campbell hadn't jumped at the chance to go with him — the best catch in the township. Instead she'd chosen to marry a man who at that time didn't have an acre of land in his name.

"Get to the point, Sam," Rachael said. "Neither of us are time wasters. That's one way we are alike."

"All right. You asked for it and here it is. The newcomers never are going to get the upper hand up at the church. There's some that will see to that. And folks like you and Tilda are just prolonging things."

Rachael smiled and shook her head. "How *can* you say that? If anyone at Willow Bend has stayed neutral it's Tilda and I."

"Humph," Sam snorted. "You call being friendly to them transplanted city people being neutral? You're just helping them got control — get the upper hand."

"You've used that term twice. And there's the nub of all this trouble. Someone, or some group, wanting to control the congregation. Do you want to know what I really think — but of course you don't. Well you're going to hear it anyway. It's God who should have the upper hand."

Sam took off his felt hat and slapped it against his thigh. Little puffs of dust came from his moleskin work trousers. He seemed to instantly regret using the hat as an implement for venting his anger. He carefully re-creased the crown with the edge of his hand and ran two fingers around the rim. Then he turned and strode toward the orange truck. The motor roared, tires spun, and gravel splattered as he headed down the Macedonia Pike.

Ordinarily Rachael would have been upset by such a confrontation. Anger, dissension, and dominating tendencies wounded her spirit and disturbed her mind. But this time she was able to go about her work in a remarkably serene state of mind. She didn't understand why she was so unruffled. "I'll have to figure that out later. Now it's time to peel potatoes and make hard sauce for the bread pudding."

She told David about Sam's visit as they ate. "I'm not surprised," her son said. "I figured Sam would be out beating the bushes for signers today. Time's running out."

"It'd be like Sam to do some agitating on the day of the prayer sessions."

The circle of the redemptive group widened to include three more people that night. Rachael wasn't surprised to see Mr. and Mrs. Laine, but her heart quickened when young Tim walked in with his parents. This was good. Young people should feel, or be made to feel, they were an integral part of the church.

Before they entered the circle of chairs Kenneth said. "We should be grateful to Ann Brooks for the fact that Tim is with us. She told me of a discussion she and Dave had with him on the way home from youth meeting last night. Do you want to tell us a little about that, Ann?"

"Yes, I do," Ann said. "Mainly because Tim gave me an idea for the theme, or text, of tonight's meditation."

She went on to tell that the devotions had been on the story of the Good Samaritan and as usual the pertinent question was "Who is my neighbor?"

"Then just before we drove into Candlewood Hills," Ann said, "Tim took a deep breath and said. 'It sure is confusing around here. Knowing whose neighbor is who. With so many people being mad.' "

"That made us realize that young people are more aware of situations than some adults realize and that they're hurt by them," Ann said.

"And the theme!" Kenneth prompted.

Ann opened her Bible and read from the tenth chapter of Luke. When she finished she said, "I felt that if we discussed the meaning of compassion we would have a better understanding of the Christ message in this parable."

The discussion went on for over an hour. Ideas were exchanged and supplemented with other views. The various interpretations seemed to stimulate thought. Rachael had the feeling that light was all around them.

By the time they joined in the benediction the up-lifted feeling seemed to be unanimous. As before no one spoke as they left the room.

Rachael had driven to Willow Bend because David worked until seven to finish planting the field of corn. He was afraid he'd be late.

Tilda had planned to ride home with Connie and the Laines, but she quickly accepted Rachael's offer of a ride.

As Mrs. Barley shut the car door she said, "I jumped at the chance to ride with you even if it does take you out of your way. But I had something to tell you. Something good."

"I'm listening," Rachael said.

"Well, you know our talk about helping the preacher?"

"Yes."

"I found a way. No, *I* didn't find it. It was sort of dumped in my lap. Today."

She went on to say that a lady from over by Springport had come to see her. Ann's aunt had given her directions.

"This Mrs. Deavers wanted to pick out colors for a rug. Well, we got to gabbing like we'd known each other all our lives. She happened to mention that she'd ordered new living-room furniture. She wants a rose rug to put in front of her couch. The new stuff's to be delivered as soon as she finds a place to store her other furniture."

"Why doesn't she sell it?" Rachael asked.

"I put the same question to her," Tilda said. "The answer was that it was too good to sell for a little or nothing. This lady seems to be well supplied with money and buys whole rooms of new furniture about as often as you and I get new shoes. She just holds on to the stuff until she finds a need to fill."

"You suggested Ken," Rachael said.

"I sure did. Quicker than a wink. It's not right. Him up there in that lonesome place with nothing but a bed, dresser, one easy chair, and kitchen stuff."

"When's he going to get it, or will he take it?" Rachael asked.

"He will. We went to see him, Mrs. Deavers and I. So Ken asked me to ride along and look at the things.

87

It's real nice. A maple sofa that opens into a bed. And a recliner chair and even a desk. Ken's going to put it in the dining room. It'll just fill it up right. That's what he was talking to your Dave about before the meeting. To ask to borrow his truck."

Rachael had turned the key and they'd talked while sitting in the car. Crickets clicked in the tall grass in the side ditch. And an owl's hollow cry came from the direction of the cedar trees.

"This *is* good news, Tilda," Rachael said. "It can't help but make the parsonage seem more like a home. I guess good is really going on."

"It always is," Tilda said. "It always is."

13/

Rachael wished several times during the next few days that she could find an excuse for not going to the meeting of the Women's Circle. "But I can't convince myself that there's a good reason for missing. And I *am* the secretary."

Lena Burke was the hostess and that meant that Cora and Sam Clinton's wife, and all who were like-minded, would attend. *Tilda and I may be in another minority,* Rachael thought as she pressed the lavender shirtwaist dress she finished the night before. *Connie may not be able to leave her mother with the children.* Mrs. Endicott was almost well. The broken hip had been slow to mend but even so it had healed sooner than the quarrel that started over the hydrangea. That was nearly eleven months ago.

"The meeting will probably be a cut-and-dried affair," Tilda said after Rachael picked her up, headed south, and branched off on to the county-line road. "Cora's got the lesson this month and you won't have to listen too close to hear the sharp digs she'll work in here and there."

"Maybe so. Maybe not," Rachael said. "What I've

been wondering about is this. Have Cora and the others heard about Lucy being in the hospital? Will they say anything?"

"If they don't, will you?" Tilda asked.

"No," Rachael said. "I couldn't go against Lucy's wishes. Besides, she's supposed to get home today."

"I know," Tilda said. "I'm figuring on trotting over that way tomorrow to see if there's anything that needs doing. If not, I can hook on a rug in her easy chairs the same as in my own."

As they rounded the bend that brought them within sight of the Burke farm Tilda said, "My land alive! Look there would you at all the cars!"

"There are more than usual," Rachael said. She parked at the end of the line on the concrete driveway. This was one of the few farms that didn't have a graveled lane. There'd been a lot of talk about how Lena used the inheritance from her father. She'd built the seven-room limestone house, put chain link fence around the yard and barn lot, and hired a paving firm to resurface the gravel drive. The general opinion was that her brother Sam and her husband had fought this waste of good money. And some others wondered what had got into Lena, what made her different from the other Clintons, who'd have been smart and bought more land.

Lena met them at the door of the screened-in porch. She had what Tilda called a bottled-up look. "Didn't you ever notice how she keeps doing things to herself? Patting her neck or rubbing one temple. Like she has to adjust something to keep herself from flying to smithereens."

"Come on in," Lena said. "If you can get in."

90

"She always says that," Rachael thought. "As if her house wasn't so orderly you'd think no one lived in it."

"It's pretty quiet in there. Has the meeting started?" Tilda said. "It's not time."

"No. Oh, no," Lena answered. "I guess they've not got limbered up yet. Of course there are several strangers."

"Strangers?" Tilda said.

Lena's pale blue eyes shifted from Rachael's face to Tilda's. Then she looked away and said, "You know — the people from Fred Marsh's cow pasture."

A flush came over Rachael's face. She could feel the warmth. She'd heard this term for Candlewood Hills before. In a way it was an accurate label. Fawn and white Guernsey cows had grazed over the rolling acreage before it was divided into lots and sold. It wasn't the name which was ridiculing. Just the tone in which it was spoken.

The long narrow living room was edged with chairs and only four were not taken. Rachael nodded to everyone in general but wasn't able to single out anyone in particular until she was seated. Then she recognized the fact that there were at least seven people from the housing project, besides Connie James. One was Mrs. Laine and Rachael had met the two others on her visits along the winding drives.

Sue Hart, the circle president, was flipping the pages of a plastic-backed notebook. She glanced at the brass sunburst clock above the gold velvet couch and then nodded to Connie.

"I asked Sue to signal me before taking up the meeting," Connie said. "As you see I brought several guests

— *after* I notified Lena, naturally. And rather than introduce them over and over whenever someone came I'm happy to do so now." She asked the visitors to stand and tell their names. Then Connie walked to each member and touched them as they were presented to the new people. It was the kind of personal move few people could do with poise, especially in a situation where feelings were intense and relations strained. But Connie had that kind of nature. Rachael had often thought the word ameliorate defined this quality of the slender young mother's character. Her presence seemed to make things better.

Some members smiled and said things like nice to meet you, glad to have you, and even, you're needed. But others merely nodded. And Cora Landess left the room before Connie came within three chairs of her. Rachael heard water running and the clink of glass on porcelain. "Cora sure got thirsty all of a sudden," Tilda whispered.

The meeting went as Mrs. Barley predicted until it came time for new business to be discussed. Sue asked if anyone had any new ideas or projects to bring before the group. Rachael thought of several things which needed doing but doubted if the circle was the right instrument for accomplishment.

"Well," Sue said. "If you don't, I do. No one here needs to be told that we have a new minister. Most of you know his salary. It has been brought to my attention that he needs a new suit. I doubt if he can afford to buy one now while he is in school. I wondered how the members would feel about using some of our funds. You heard the treasurer's report. We have more than $186.

No one spoke for what seemed like a very long time. Then Tilda said, "Seems like a right idea to me. I'd be for it.

Connie James said, "I agree. My vote would be aye."

Then Cora Landess came back into the room. Even before she sat down she said, "I'd vote *nay*. This man's not been here long enough to tell if he's going to work out or not. How do we know he's going to earn what he gets?"

She means how does she know he's going to line up with the right side, Rachael thought.

"More'n that," Mrs. Sam Clinton said, "is it fitting for preachers to expect handouts all the time? The rest of us didn't get what we got that way."

Didn't they? Rachael thought. *Big Joe Clinton's money gave all four of his children a big boost.*

Sue Hart's face was pale. Rachael knew that the president regretted bringing up the subject. A quick count convinced her that a motion to buy the suit would not carry. The visitors were not members yet and could not vote. She was ashamed that they were hearing the selfish, uncharitable remarks.

A flood of thoughts rushed into her mind as she cleared her throat and said, "Madam President, I'd like to say something." Her words came slowly at first, as if she had to guide them through the churning channel of her feelings. "I'm the secretary of this circle. I record the business of these meetings. I'd not feel happy or right if it became necessary for me to go home tonight and write that the majority of the members of this church-related group voted against filling this need. It would be painful for me to read the report of this action at next month's meeting. It's bad enough to swallow a bitter pill once. To have to do it twice would leave a bad taste with me for a long time. So I move that this idea be tabled."

After the motion was quickly seconded and shoved into a vote Rachael again asked for the floor. "I'm sure that in the Willow Bend congregation or even in this room there is enough kindness and compassion to see that our minister has a suit. I for one, as an individual, will start the fund by giving Mrs. Hart some money after the meeting. Is that all right with you, Sue?"

"It certainly is, Rachael. Thank you."

After the benediction Tilda reached over and put one hand on Rachael's wrist. "Good for you! I like spunk."

Inwardly Rachael had misgivings. Had she increased tension? Made things worse? She looked around the room as Cora, Lena, and Mrs. Clinton began to serve refreshments. Some people were chattering in little groups. Others moved from one cluster of chairs to another. The air seemed to be cleared. People, or most of them, were at ease.

Sue brought the glass serving tray, with the cup of lemonade and dish of crushed strawberries on angel cake, to a chair next to Rachael's. As they ate and talked several people stopped to give money to Mrs. Hart. They didn't slip folded bills into Sue's palm or slide it under the ridged tray on her lap. They gave it openly, freely, and didn't seem to care that Cora Landess watched from the other side of the room.

"You in any hurry to get home, Tilda?" Rachael asked as they started back toward Willow Bend.

"No. I reckon not," Tilda said. "Everything that's

waiting to be done will be there when I get back."

"Well, I just thought you might have a rush order to fill before Ann goes to Newcastle tomorrow."

"No. I'm all caught up on orders. Tomorrow I'll work toward getting ahead again. Why? What's on your mind?"

"Oh, I was thinking we might go calling on our shut-in members. Kenneth mentioned that he wished we could carry church to them in some way. I said I'd try to find out what they missed most. So we'd have something to go on when he began figuring out what could be done — and how."

"I'd like that," Tilda said. They rode for a full mile in silence before she added. "Have you realized how much is going on, Rachael? A few more people seem interested in church. Sue collecting enough for a fairly good suit of clothes. Ken's furniture. And this idea about shut-ins. D'you reckon this redemptive thing is working?"

"Could be," Rachael said.

They visited three homes before the sun sank into a bed of clouds which looked like rosy smoke. One lady lived in a house trailer behind her son's home and was well cared for, but lonely. She missed the music most. "Sometimes I take off singing all by myself. But *Blest Be the Tie That Binds* don't sound the same when there's only one. And I'm not the kind that enjoys my own voice. It doesn't inspire me much."

The second stop was at Frank Granger's, who hadn't walked a step since the tractor upset and pinned him to the bottom of a rock-strewn ravine for four hours before anyone found him. Frank was glum and almost unfriendly. "And not about to bare his feeling to any do-gooder women," Tilda said afterward.

Then Rachael happened (or so it seemed) to mention that her son David had bought a harness horse. Frank's eyes brightened. "Horses are pretty animals. Move like water flowing. Maybe a lot of us'd be better off if we'd stuck to horsepower."

Rachael saw one way to brighten Frank's days. It might not have any connection with the ministry of the church. But it wouldn't be contrary to any of God's laws if she asked David to ride up and let the crippled man see the chestnut pacer. He might even coax him to go for a ride in the yellow-wheeled cart.

As they pulled in Tilda's drive she said, "They all miss different things, the music, the sermons — but even if they didn't say it I have the feeling that most of all they missed being with folks."

"I think you're right," Rachael said. "I'm sure Frank would like seeing Victor. But deep down he'd get more good out of having David, or anyone, take time to visit him."

14

By the time of the next prayer session Rachael was aware of a change in her own attitude and thinking. A kind of alteration had taken place. "It could be that I'm just too busy to spend time worrying and thinking about whether the church will survive," she thought.

A strong summer breeze had loosened the hold of many mealy transparent apples on the tree. Rachael was filling a plastic bucket with the fruit. She meant to share them with Tilda who often said, "I can make a scrumptious meal of bread, butter, and warm applesauce."

As she worked she looked backward on the week. The Friday cooking class, the Women's Circle meeting, Monday's session, and the visits to the shut-ins had brought a new tempo to her life. *And there's a sense of harmony to what's going on.*

She cautioned herself against building up too much hope. "It could be just wishful thinking on my part, but I see signs of recovering what we'd lost at Willow Bend. Some, anyway." The same people refused to speak to the same. And the Coras and Sams bypassed shaking the preacher's hand if they could find a way around him. But the coolness and rude behavior hadn't been so noticeable the Sunday before. Most of the Candlewood Hills ladies, who'd been at the Women's Circle meeting, brought their families to church. They made a sizable delegation. Several regular members hurried to make them feel welcome. Rachael wasn't the lone member of the welcoming committee.

Kenneth made another positive move that morning. He took off his glasses as he made the announcement. "I've studied the rosters of the Sunday school classes this week. I was surprised and challenged to learn that the high school age class has the longest list of names. Now, as you know, this doesn't show up on the attendance board. But the potential is there. They do come often enough to get their name on the book at least once every quarter. Some adults attend as infrequently.

"I'd like to draw more deeply on this source. Any effort cannot be expected to succeed if all the resources are not tapped. And this class, *The Challengers*, is an important segment of the total church."

He went on to say that he was asking each class to meet with him on successive Sunday evenings. "I'm hoping this will lead to reestablishment of Sunday evening worship services. But for now the purpose will be to assess the feeling of each group on how to enrich our fellowship. So, since there are more Challengers than any other group, I'd like to see them an hour before the regular Youth Group meeting next Sunday night — at five o'clock."

Rachael felt that Ken had made another invigorating move. But she also realized that Sam Clinton would oppose the spreading of any new idea which might loosen his hold on the reins.

Suddenly she thought, "What happened to that remonstrance? I haven't heard a word. I'll have to ask David."

Her son and his wife were away for the day attending a retreat for lay people at the college in Wayne County. She'd not had a chance to ask about how Sam's plan to block the addition to the school had gone until that morning. Then they had several other things to discuss before Dave went to the field.

After the apples were gathered from the carpet of grass Rachael began to get ready to go to church. She was tightening a button on her lavender dress when someone said "Yoo-hoo," from the back steps.

"Tilda Barley — how'd you get here? Walk?"

"Part way," Tilda said. "Sue Hart stopped on the way from Muncie. I'd sent for four more yards of burlap for my rugmaking. So I hitched a ride. She wanted to bring me on down. But she had supper to get. Besides, I need the limbering up."

"Come on in," Rachael said. "You eaten.?"

"Oh, sure. Had a mess of new peas. They're doing real good. All that rain, you know."

"You are going to church, aren't you?"

"Yes. Wouldn't miss. But I heard something today. I just had to tell you."

"Good?"

"Good and sort of mystical," Tilda said. "See! You've got me to using that word. It's about Lottie Springer. You don't reckon anyone's told her about how we joined in hunting ways to help Ken, do you?"

"Oh, I doubt it," Rachael said. "It's sort of generally

understood that it's not fair to put the Springers in the position of taking sides — because they're in business."

"They need all the trade they can get to keep their heads above water," Tilda added.

"But I don't understand," Rachael said. "How can you connect Lottie with a move you think she couldn't know anything about?"

"That's where the mystical part comes in," Tilda said. "But let me begin at the start. You got time to listen?"

"I'll take time," Rachael said. "You've stirred up every curious cord in me. Besides, it'll be more than half an hour before Ann and David come past."

"Well," Tilda began as she sat down in the kitchen rocker. "I just happened on to what Lottie's doing. I walked up to the store for a few groceries early this morning. Ken drove up to the gasoline pumps just as I was leaving and said to wait, that he was going by my place."

She went on to say that Lottie filled up Ken's car. "I was standing so I could see the window that tells how much gas costs. It stopped at $5.94. Ken had a bill in his hand. But Lottie just smiled and walked right past him. You know the Springers don't make that kind of money."

"No. I doubt if they have much margin of profit," Rachael said. "But Lottie's good-hearted. And, of course, we don't know that she hasn't done the same for other ministers."

"No. I guess we don't," Tilda admitted. "There are some who don't give so as to be seen before men."

"That's right," Rachael said.

"But it's still surprising. Lottie and Art haven't attended church for, my goodness, I can't remember how long! Did something happen? Do you recall?"

"No," Rachael said. "I remember when Lottie went to the Women's Circle and was in my Sunday school class. But she never breathed a word of anger at anyone — at least not to me."

By the time 7:30 came nineteen of the twenty-four chairs in the parsonage living room had been taken. Kenneth Holden smiled and said, "It's going to take some crowding to make a circle within this rectangular room."

"Maybe it's about time we took our place in the church basement," Brad James said.

"That could be. We'll think about that."

Tim Laine came again, but not with his parents. He brought two friends. One was a smiling boy with copper hair, and to everyone's amazement the other was pretty Lori Landess, Cora's daughter.

In the noise of moving to form the circle Tilda said, "I wonder if her mamma knows she's here?"

Connie James smiled and said, "Some things go on in spite of Cora's prejudices. Like Lori dating Tim."

"So that's the way the land lies," Tilda said.

Kenneth led the discussion. "Last week our text or theme came from a youth group meeting. I'm drawing on a personal experience and suggesting that we talk more about the parable of the Good Samaritan. We didn't explore it fully last week. There have been several good neighbors in my time at Willow Bend. They've bound up my wounds and taken care of various needs. Mainly these acts of compassion have been performed by members of the congregation. I'm grateful and touched and

101

comforted. But this week a need was filled by someone I've not seen in church, whose name has not been on the rolls for nearly twenty-one years. This led me into a deeper search for the answer to the question, "Who *is* my neighbor?"

He means Lottie Springer. Rachael glanced at Tilda who smiled and nodded.

Just as Kenneth called on Sue Hart for an expression of opinion someone rapped on the door. Ann Brooks hurried to open it for Lucy Cavanaugh.

"I'm sorry to barge in late," she said. "But I couldn't find my car keys."

She was pale but seemed unusually calm.

"We're glad you came," Kenneth said. "It's good to have you with us." Then he smiled. "Lucy's been away — in the hospital in Henry County. She needed a rest and the few of us who knew where she was respected her wish to have a quiet time."

The group discussed the meaning of the Samaritan story for over an hour. Everyone participated, even Lori Landess. She said, "I used to think only people on every side of us were really neighbors. But they're not always — not helpful, or even kind to each other."

One thought was repeated over and over. Anyone who shows mercy is a neighbor.

"It's getting late I know," Mrs. Laine said. "But would it be possible for us to discuss the word mercy sometime?"

"Why not next week?" the minister said. "This is good — one discussion leading into the next. Like a unifying chord."

Rachael wondered if Lori and the red-haired boy

would join the prayer circle. Would they feel out of place, or not in harmony with a group of adults? But someone, either Ken or Tim or both had prepared them for the procedure. They were receptive and reverent. Tears streamed down Lori's cheeks as she rose from her place. *Poor child. She's had enough of hate. Too much probably.*

David Brooks was ready to slide behind the steering wheel when Brad James hurried across the church parking lot. "Are you busy evenings, now?" he asked.

"No. Not at the present," David said. "When I get into haymaking the baler runs until dew falls. Why?"

"Well, Tom Laine's got someplace he wants us to go one evening this week."

"Let me know," David said.

"I wonder what that's all about?" Ann asked. "Do you know?"

"No. Not for sure. But I'd be willing to hazard a guess that it's something about a car."

"What makes you think that?" Ann asked.

"No mystery," David said. "Mr. Laine runs three filling stations in the city, and one's connected with a garage."

"You think this has something to do with Kenneth and a car, don't you?" Rachael asked.

"Could be," her son said. "Could be."

The world seemed especially lovely to Rachael. The moonlight was like veiled silver. She could see the trickling water as they crossed the Cabin Creek bridge. The willows on the bank were feathery, and frosted by the night light.

As David slowed the car and coasted to a stop Ann

said, "Why don't you go home with us, Rachael? Stay all night."

"Oh, I might as well stay —" Then something prompted her to ask. "Why, Ann? Is there a special reason?"

"No. Not any need," Ann said. "But when I leave the prayer circle my heart's so full of love and tenderness that I don't want to say good-bye to you. I want us to stay together a little longer. Besides, you never have in all these four years."

Rachael's eyes filled with tears. She reached over and squeezed Ann's hand. "That's reason enough for me. I'll get some things and lock up a little tighter."

"I'll do that for you, Mom" David said.

15/

Rachael rode home in her son's truck the next morning. This was the day David planned to get the mower out of the tool shed on the home farm and cut the alfalfa in the field along Cabin Creek. No rain was expected, according to the radio forecast, for at least five days. That would be enough time to let the hay dry before it was raked, baled, and stowed in the loft in the barn.

As summer crept closer to autumn the green of the foliage deepened. Rachael saw this change in the leaves on the redbud tree as she walked around the house to make her daily inspection of the garden. The green fingers of the Top Crop beans were almost big enough to be picked; and heads were forming in the cluster of fan-shaped cabbage leaves.

I'd better get out and do some weed-pulling before the sun gets high in the sky, she thought. Lamb's-quarter and bindweed were choking the feathery fronds of the carrots.

As she worked, a recurring observation came to her mind. It took more care and effort to pull the first weed than it did the second and each one came out with less tugging. *Isn't that the way it is with a lot of things, trying new jobs, breaking old habits?*

She thought of the second cooking class at the mission. She, as well as the four members, were more comfortable. Their efforts seemed to mesh. As one young woman put it, "I didn't feel like I had ten thumbs today."

The carrot row was free of weeds by ten-thirty. Rachael washed the green and the grit from her hands before she started the meal of spaghetti and meatballs. She was taking a half loaf of French bread from the freezer when she heard a knock on the door.

She turned and hurried to welcome Kenneth. "Well, hello! Come on in."

"Gladly," the minister said. "Something smells good!"

"It's my spaghetti sauce," Rachael said. "You willing to stay and try it? David's eating here. Otherwise I'd not be going to so much fuss."

"Was I hinting?" Ken asked.

"I don't think so — but if you were I took it. Do you want to talk or look up something?"

"Well, both. But talk's on the tip of my tongue," Kenneth said. "About what's probably on everyone's this morning."

Rachael lifted the wooden spoon from the simmering spicy sauce and looked puzzled.

"You haven't seen the morning paper?"

"No. I haven't even taken it out of the tube. What's — " Rachael asked.

"The remonstrance against the school building failed. They didn't get enough signers."

"And it's in the paper? There wasn't any meeting for a reporter to visit or have I missed something?"

Kenneth explained that someone from the *Star* had evidently heard of the controversy and had ferreted out a story. He'd questioned the township trustee and one member of the advisory board. "They seemed to duck from answering questions directly," Ken said. "And they must have told the newsman to see Sam Clinton."

"And Sam talked," Rachael said.

"He did. Plenty."

"Was it bad? Of course I'll read it later *if* I can stand to see the ugly words. They *were* insulting? Am I right?"

"They were," Ken said. "About what you'd expect. A lot about city folks sponging on founding families. Expecting others to build schools for their kids. Bringing radical ideas into the community."

"Did he use the term communistic?" Rachael asked.

"I don't remember seeing it. Sam *couldn't* think that of anyone we know," Ken said.

"Oh, yes. He *could* and does. Of course," Rachael added, "Sam may not be able to define the word. But that doesn't keep him from using it. Frequently."

"I wonder," Ken asked as Rachael crumbled browned ground meat into the bubbling sauce. "Will this affect the church?"

"It's hard to tell for sure," she said. "I don't really have anything on which to base a guess. I don't recall Sam ever being beaten before. I'm not sure how he'll act or react."

"I don't have to guess," Ken said. "I know one thing Mr. Clinton's going to do in retaliation."

He went on to say that he'd been in the general store early that morning. "Mrs. Springer told me that she'd heard Sam talking to someone. She'd taken papers and boxes to the trash barrel. It seems these men were on the other side of the elderberry bushes working on a tractor. The way Mrs. Springer put it, there was as much clanging and banging in Sam's voice as there was in the use of the tools."

Rachael sat down on one of the kitchen chairs. Her lips curved in a half smile as Ken talked. "Sam's going to quit paying into the church," she said.

Kenneth shook his head in amazement. "How did you know that?"

"That's not a mystery. Sam's been threatening to withhold his support for years. He's a big contributor. That's true. There's no doubt the Clinton money has helped keep Willow Bend's door open. But I'm not sure that's a healthy financial condition, let alone being good for the spiritual life."

"So?" Ken asked. "What do you think will happen? You don't seem alarmed."

"No. I'm not. I've never been in favor of knuckling under just because Sam wanted his own way. He never changed my vote with that kind of threat. That's too much like blackmail."

She told of the time when a pastor had tried to get the church to adopt a new project. He'd worked in a mission school in the South for a year and wanted to keep on helping the boys he'd known.

"All he wanted," Rachael, said, "was for us to assume the responsibility of clothing the eight boys in one cottage. It seemed like a good idea to most of us. But not to Sam. He wasn't going to encourage shiftlessness and give no-good parents the idea that hardworking people up here could be bled."

"And it was voted down?" Ken asked.

"It was never even brought to a vote. Not before the congregation. Sam wielded the club of his money in a board meeting when I wasn't there. That was the year of John's last illness."

"The situation's not quite the same now," Ken said. "The remonstrance wasn't blocked in the church."

"No. But he probably blames the newcomers and people like me. So he's acting in spite. Trying to hold on to any rein of control. But somehow I'm hopeful. His grip may be loosened there too."

"Well," Ken said. "I hope so. The word church boss is heard a lot in seminary school. The idea of one-man or one-woman domination is one that seems to splinter many congregations."

"Or fracture them," Rachael said.

David Brooks hurried to the mailbox as soon as he heard the news. He read the article aloud as Rachael chopped tomatoes and radishes for the tossed salad.

"Well, what do *you* think?" she asked. "Will this hurt the church?"

David shook his head. "I doubt it. The only person who could be hurt by remarks like that is the person who made them. They come from deep-down hate and bigotry. Those feelings are with Sam all the time."

Rachael smiled to herself after Kenneth went to the living room to do some research, and David went to the field. "I can almost hear the telephone wires humming and wouldn't be a bit surprised to learn that traffic was heavier than usual around here today." She tried to stifle the impulse to go see Tilda and discuss the latest happening. They'd lived through so many up and down times. *If this is to be a turning point I'd like to share it with her.*

Mrs. Barley evidently had the same feeling. She came around the corner of the house as Rachael pinned three bleached dish towels on the wire clothesline.

"You don't look one bit surprised to see me."

"Would you have been to see me?" Rachael asked.

"No," Tilda said. "And I would have stayed at home and waited. But Connie James came by."

"Why didn't she come in?" Rachael asked.

"She'll stop by later. She's taking her little ones to a birthday party somewheres on the other side of the schoolhouse."

"Want to go in the house? On second thought I believe we'd better sit out here. Kenneth's looking up something. Our chatter might disturb him."

"I guess he walked," Tilda said.

"Yes. Probably to save his car."

Tilda shook her head. "That automobile of his reminds me of the story that used to be in our readers, 'The Wonderful One Horse Shay.'"

"That fell apart all at once," Rachael said. "I remember it well."

They sat in the shade of the Yellow Transparent apple tree. The sun had moved over the rooftop and was shining down on the west side of the house. The big tractor was moving around a section of the hayfield. Rachael hoped that all dogs and wild animals were out of the path of the sharp-toothed sickle. It cut a wide swath.

Tilda sniffed the air. "That's the cleanest smell there is," she said. "I wish I could bottle some up. It might sell. I could call it *New-Mown Hay*."

"Or *Aroma of Alfalfa*," Rachael said.

"You got a real peaceful look on your face. Hadn't you heard?"

"About Sam shutting his pocketbook as far as Willow Bend's concerned? I heard. You don't seem too upset yourself."

Tilda smiled. "Nope. Actually I'm relieved. I've been curious about something for a long long spell. I'd like to find out if Willow Bend can survive."

"Survive *and* thrive," Rachael said. "That's what I'd like to see."

At this moment the minister came out of the house. "Well! I've been wanting to talk to both of you at once. About your visits to the shut-ins. Did you come to any conclusions on how the church can include them in its ministry?"

Rachael told him that maybe a tape recorder could be used to carry the sermons and music to some. Then the idea of a plan of regular visitation might brighten the lives of all who were confined to their homes.

"Not any of these now-and-then calls," Tilda said. "They need something to look forward to. I try to picture how I'd be if I thought no one was likely to stop by. I'd probably get so I wouldn't even bother to put on a clean apron."

"I wonder how this kind of ministry should start?" Kenneth said. "With the official board or the prayer group. Or should it be brought up before the whole congregation?"

"How about these meetings you're going to have with the Sunday classes?" Rachael asked. "Perhaps they would be a good source of ideas."

"Fine," Kenneth said. He was quiet for a while. Then he smiled and said, "Wouldn't this be an extension of the idea of small redemptive groups?"

"Looks like they're horses of the same color," Tilda said. "To my way of thinking that's fine. The leaven of good is working."

"You think so?" Ken asked.

"I do," Tilda said.

"And I agree," Rachael added. "There's a new feeling here. I can't describe or define it. But something's working, as Tilda said. Or being allowed to work."

16/

Rachael didn't talk to or see anyone in the neighborhood except her family and two Candlewood Hills boys until Saturday afternoon. The sun dried the windrows of green alfalfa into crisp and fragrant hay. David went over to the housing project and hired Tim Laine and a friend to help him bale and store the forage crop for winter feed.

The three haymakers worked until nearly dark, until misty dew began to settle on the prairie. Rachael cooked both a noon and evening meal, knowing that the families who'd moved out from town ate many hours before nine o'clock. The boys would miss their supper at home.

At the end of the day, Tim and his friend chugged and hummed down the Macedonia Pike on their motorbikes. The first evening Rachael asked her son, "How'd they do?"

"Well enough," David said. "Of course, they have to be told a lot. But these two are willing to listen. That redheaded kid had blisters on his palms. I know they hurt. But he didn't let up."

"Do you think they'll be back tomorrow?"

"Yes. The idea of earning money is an inducement. Besides I think they're bored. Tim told me that Candlewood Hills is kind of a trap sometimes. Far enough out of town so they can't go to the Y or shows or places."

"Some do," Rachael said. "Connie James said she dreaded for her little ones to get out from under her feet. Someone's always coaxing her neighbor boys to go wandering."

"I suppose the same type people are there as here," David said. "Some care about their kids. Some don't. But in the housing project they *are* sort of penned up — close together. That makes problems."

Ann came down and cooked for the haymakers on Friday so that Rachael wouldn't have to miss the cooking class. She wasn't sure that this venture would, or should, go on indefinitely. She'd begun to see that there wouldn't be enough people to make it a full-time project. After this six-week session it might be a while before this need became apparent again. *But I'd be willing to do it again. If I'm asked.*

The hayfield was raked clean and the crop was stored by four o'clock on Friday evening. Rachael saw the bristly stubble as she crossed the Cabin Creek bridge. *Now David will probably use the rotary hoe on the cornfields to keep the weeds from getting a head start on the corn.* Jimpsonweed, butterprint, and gentian always seemed to outgrow the cultivated seeds.

The meals for extra people had depleted Rachael's food supply. So she made out a list and went up to the general store a little before Saturday noon. As soon as she walked in the door she noticed a change.

The tall heating stove was in plain view. The counter which had always held stacks of denim work clothes had been shoved to the back wall. Lottie's rocking chair was no longer out of sight from the door. Customers could see as well as hear when she tilted forward to arise from its woven seat. The two benches from the old church were empty. There were no loafers, seen or unseen.

"Morning, Rachael," Lottie said. "How are you this fine bright day?"

"Good. And you?"

"The same. The same," Lottie said.

"I can't help but notice — you've moved things around."

Lottie squinted her eyes and paused before answering. "Are you in a real big hurry?"

"No. I'm not. Why?"

"Well — I've *got* to talk to somebody," Lottie said. "I feel like a skillet that's too full of popcorn. The grains that keep exploding are liable to raise the lid. *Only* — this lid's been on for more'n twenty years."

"And you want to tell me who put it on?" Rachael said.

"Right. Clamped, bolted, and riveted tight. Of course, I didn't have to let him. Sam Clinton, I mean."

Things began to fit together in Rachael's mind. It had been that long since the Springers had attended church. But how could Sam have anything to do with them dropping out? He traded with them. In fact his voice came from behind the overall counter more than anyone's.

"You're puzzled. I can see it on your face," Lottie said. "It's hard for me to find the right place to begin to unravel this tale. It's like those sacks of salt we used

115

to get. If you pull the *right* thread the chain of stitches is unlocked and each kinked thread separates. But if you pick at the wrong ones then the going's tedious."

"And you don't know what's the right thread or who?" Rachael said.

Lottie smiled and nodded. "It's a who. My Art. That's why I've not been able to name this whole mess to a soul. Because of shame maybe. And partly pity — or mercy."

She went on to tell that Sam Clinton had wound her husband around his little finger two decades ago. The Springers lived on one of the Clinton tenant farms. They worked for monthly wages and lived in a house that was "one big draft when the wind blew," as Lottie put it.

"Sam took to Art in a way. Hauled him around to sales and to town. But all the time he was just buttering him up. Getting him sharpened like a tool for his own uses."

It seemed that Sam had bought a stockyards over in Randolph County. He put Art Springer in as sort of manager. "That's what Sam *said*," Lottie told Rachael. "But the truth was that he needed a flunky, someone who'd look at the scales from the wrong angle. And Art did. He was that hungry to get ahead. But they got caught."

"I never heard anything about this," Rachael said.

"You nor no one else. The weight inspector, or whoever the big shot was, wanted to get ahead fast too. And Sam's never lacked for money to cover the crooked deals he made trying to make more money."

"But Sam comes in here. And he goes to church,"

Rachael said. "Why did you —"

"Why did *we* quit?" Lottie said. "Well. I guess the only way to explain it is to say that people's consciences come in all shapes and sizes and states. We couldn't fit ours into doing as Sam did. And as for him trading with us — I guess he's still afraid Art might get up spunk and tell on him."

She told that they'd moved off Sam's land when the time of Art's hiring came to an end. They'd saved a little money, borrowed a little, and bought the Willow Bend store. It gave them a place to live after they made the upper floor into four rooms. They'd made a living and whittled a thin shaving off the chunk of their debt every year.

"But it seems so sad — so lonely that you sort of withdrew from the rest of us," Rachael said. "Art never really profited from the short weights."

"No," Lottie said. "But that's where the conscience thing comes into the picture again. He knew he was wrong. He knows it now. He's whipped himself all these years. Didn't you ever wonder why he's so fidgety?"

"I've noticed, but thought it was his nature to be on the go."

"No," Lottie said. "He just thinks too much if he sits. Once in a real bad time he confessed that Sam had promised him a $500 bonus if he could manage things so they wouldn't get caught. So Art feels as guilty as if that money had really changed hands."

Sue Hart's little girl came in for a loaf of bread and a carton of milk, giving Rachael time to think over what she'd heard. When Lottie came back to the bench she asked, "Why did you tell me this and why today?"

"The first part of your question's easy to answer. I know you won't tell. As for the second part, that's hard to explain. It's like something sort of mysterious is going on. Like a changing. You know, like before a summer shower is coming, you can smell the rain before you feel a drop."

"Yes. I know," Rachael says. "It's like when you sense spring in the air even if there's still snow on the ground."

"Or get the feel of winter at a certain time in August," Lottie said. "Without even thinking about a calendar."

"I suppose we pass landmarks without actually seeing them," Rachael said. "But we know we've covered ground. Did this have anything to do with you moving the counter?"

Lottie bit her lip. "Yes it did. Now that you mention it. The day I read Sam didn't get his way about the school the notion to change things took root. I didn't want this place to be one of his dark and hidden corners. Not anymore. In a way his power has ended. *I hope.*"

"I understand," Rachael said. "Well I'd better get my groceries and get on home."

Lottie helped her carry the purchases to the car. Willow Bend was quiet. Sue Hart's hand washing was slapping in the breeze. A power lawn mower was chuffing down the street. The boys' voices came from the basketball court beyond Hart's garage.

Rachael hated to leave Lottie. She had this inner feeling that Mrs. Springer was clinging to her. Why? Was it stored-up loneliness? Or was there something else on her mind?

Suddenly without realizing why, she said, "Lottie, have

you heard about the Monday night prayer circle? Would you — could you come?"

Tears filled Mrs. Springer's brown eyes. She hurried to blot them with the corner of her white muslin apron. She worked to regain control and then she said, "I'd heard. Sue told me. And maybe that's the root of the truth about why I wanted to talk to you."

"Then you will come?"

"I want to. Worst way. But it'll not be easy to walk in and face people. Wondering what they think or guess."

Rachael said that she doubted if anyone in the prayer group would make Lottie feel uneasy or out of place. She told that Lucy Cavanaugh came, timidly at first. And that Lori Landess had been present the last time. "I can see that it would be hard to walk into church after all this time. But the prayer meetings might be a stepping-stone. Would you like to go with me Monday evening?"

"I'd appreciate that," Lottie said. "I'm a big baby maybe, or a coward. But it'd be easier if I wasn't alone."

"Do you think Art will object?" Rachael asked.

Lottie said that she'd begun to think her husband's guilt feelings would be relieved if he didn't feel that his actions were keeping her from doing what gave her comfort. "At the time I felt obliged to be loyal to him. To do as he did. But that might not have been the way to help him."

Rachael started the car and was ready to turn around and head home. She looked at the sacks of groceries in the backseat. There was nothing which would melt or be hurt in any way if it wasn't put away for an hour or so.

She turned west at the end of the street, drove for

two miles before crossing the state highway. The entrance to Candlewood Hills was a mile and a half west. She could easily recall when all this part of the township was farmland. Now the four-lane highway, the row of tapering utility towers, and the housing project had taken big chunks out of fields that once grew corn, oats, wheat, and soybeans.

Suddenly Rachael missed the barns. In the three-mile stretch only one was standing. Some had been torn down and replaced by garages. Houses were built in two places. A tall concrete silo stood like a watchtower on the Cooper place. It was not as easy to tear down as framed barns.

It's change, Rachael thought as she pulled in the driveway at the James' home. *It goes on all the time. And always has. Some adjust, other's fight it.*

She walked to the door and hoped what Tilda heard was correct. *If Mrs. Endicott is out of her wheelchair maybe she'll go home with me. No need to confine myself to Willow Bend as long as I can venture beyond its boundaries now and then. If city and country people are jammed together I don't see any reason why we can't be friends.*

17/

The annual Brooks family reunion was being held in Richmond that Sunday. Ann and David were taking Rachael. She'd hurried around that morning cooking lemon pie filling, browning the swirls of meringue, and turning flour-dredged pieces of chicken until they were crusty brown.

In a way these gatherings made her sad. It wasn't that John's folks made her feel unwanted now that he was gone. But it wasn't the same without him. Empty places reappeared. Aching spots became more sensitive.

But David's a Brooks. And he'd miss me. Besides I'll adjust as the day goes on. I always do.

She rode to church that morning. They were leaving as soon as worship service was over. They'd miss Sunday school, which was unusual.

The congregation had risen to sing the first song when Rachael slipped in her seat. Tilda smiled and handed her a songbook opened to *Have Thine Own Way, Lord.*

After the responsive reading, Kenneth made the usual announcements. Then he said, "The board meeting will be postponed for one week — for a reason. Being fairly new here, I'd like to know more about the feelings of the whole congregation. I'm thinking of the possibility of having Sunday school at 9:30. There are other matters which should concern all of you. Therefore, I'd like to have a general discussion meeting this Thursday, instead of the board meeting. Possible changes will be discussed. Then when the official group performs its duties it will know how all of us think."

"Sam's not going to like that," Rachael thought. "He's either been a steward or trustee for years and not been crossed very often."

She glanced toward the end of the side pew. Sam's place was empty. For a moment Rachael's breath seemed to catch in her throat. She had trouble controlling her thoughts. Was Sam sick? He never had been for as long as she could remember. He might be staying away in anger, to emphasize his vow to quit supporting the church. But somehow Rachael was doubtful. The old Sam would come, defiant and determined and wanting people to see he didn't put the usual crisp twenty-dollar bill in the collection plate. Some said he made special trips to the bank for those rustling bills.

Rachael had the feeling that Tilda was staring at her. She turned and smiled at her friend. *She's thinking the same thing as I am. Sam's pride is wounded. He's been whipped.*

A tinge of sadness shadowed Rachael's mind. She'd prayed that the dissension in the church would end before it split the congregation so widely no bridge would span the chasm. She'd been heartened by the evidence of the power of redemptive prayer — it was right that barriers or walls between old residents and new people, between city and country folk, be broken down. It was good that God was acting in the minds and hearts of people.

She'd seen much good. Tilda had new hope and purpose. Lucy was penitent and more receptive to His will. And the collective souls of Willow Bend were stirred to respond to needs. But did this have to result in someone being severed from church? This didn't seem right.

Rachael took a deep breath and forced herself to dismiss such thoughts before the sermon began. She'd always had the feeling that full concentration on the spoken word would have a positive effect on any listener. She'd once told Tilda, "Sometimes I'm guilty of letting my mind wander a bit. Then I think of how wasteful and impolite I'm being. The minister works hard to prepare a sermon, and we pay him to do it. So why let it go in one ear and out the other, or never listen at all?"

"I know," Tilda said. "I went home one time and couldn't even recall the text. So I sat myself down and made a list of all the things I could remember that went through my mind during that thirty or forty minutes. I'd worried if I turned off the fire under the boiling beef. I took up such subjects as the weeds in the lima beans, why my hens weren't laying, the worn soles on my shoes, and Mabel Kincaid's hat."

"Mabel's hat?" Rachael asked. "Why *it*?"

"Well, she sat in front of me that day. And I kept trying to figure out if it was new or an old one fixed over. The green velvet ribbon and pink rose looked new but the straw seemed a little yellow. Or course it could have been ivory."

"What did you do with your list?" Rachael asked.

123

"I wadded it up and burned it. The next Sunday I listened to every word in spite of Mabel's hat. She sat in front of me again."

Rachael felt a little uncomfortable leaving before Sunday school. But she did notice that more seats were filled than usual. She caught a glimpse of Cora Landess and Lena Burke. Evidently Sam's feelings hadn't kept them at home. This was good. Ridged furrows should be smoothed not scooped away.

The reunion was as Rachael expected — a light and shadow kind of experience. She moved among the groups assembled around the long green picnic tables in Glen Miller Park. Light filtered through the leaves of the canopy of trees and made trembling dappled patterns on everything within its shade. She greeted people she'd known for nearly three decades and was introduced to new additions to the families, babies, brides, and young men who'd married girls of the clan.

The most painful moment came when she met the eyes of Robert Brooks, John's only brother. The two men had been friends and the communication between them was the kind that could be established without words.

At first Rachael's throat was constricted. She sat down across from the tall gray-eyed man in the slatted swing. Finally he said, "It's been a while Rachael."

"I know. You and Sara were out West a year ago. She looks so much better."

"She is," Robert said. "David tells me you're keeping busy."

"Not a bad way to be, is it?"

"No. Idleness isn't living to my way of thinking." Neither said anything for several minutes. They watched two little boys rolling down a grassy slope. Beyond them curved-necked swans drifted across an oval pond.

"That Dave. He's a fine young man," Robert said. "More like John all the time."

"I know," Rachael said.

"But there's a lot of you in him too," Robert said. "I hear it in his talk." He went on to say that David had promised to come to Akron before the summer was over. "Sara and I won't hear to you staying at home. So hop in and come along."

After the tables were cleared the men moved to a shadier spot. Someone had a transistor radio and was tuned in on the Cincinnati Reds' baseball game.

Rachael walked to the playground with a group of women and children. As little ones slid, swung, and circled on swaying maypoles, family news was exchanged. As they talked Ann Brooks came to the end of the bench and said softly, "Would you like to walk over to the flower beds with me, Rachael?"

"Yes, I would," Rachael said. "I noticed the Cannas when we pulled in. So many lovely colors. Mine always came out red or yellow."

They strolled around every rectangular and circular bed reading the names on the stakes and comparing the flowers to their own.

Ann looked especially lovely to Rachael. Her taffy-colored hair fell into a shining crown of curls. She wore a cotton knit suit of pale peach which matched the color in her cheeks.

Rachael had turned to start back to the group when Ann said, "In a way I was selfish to ask you to come over here. To leave the others."

"Why?" Rachael said. "I've enjoyed it. You know how I love flowers and it's only natural — " Then she looked at Ann. Tears were swimming in her gentian blue eyes.

"Oh, Ann. Something's on your mind. What's wrong?"

"Nothing. Nothing's wrong. Let's sit down on the grass a minute."

Rachael's heart beat a little faster as she waited for her daughter-in-law to speak. Meaningful moments didn't catch her completely unaware. She could sense when one was near.

"I didn't mean to tell you today," Ann said. "Not when there are so many around for you to talk to."

"No one as important to me as you," Rachael said. "And David."

"*And* David," Ann echoed. "I wanted him to be in on this. And we'd planned it that way. But over there at the playground — I saw you watching Sara's little grandson — and — "

Rachael reached over and clasped Ann's wrist. "And you couldn't wait to tell me you're going to have a baby?"

"You know — "

"No. I didn't. But I do know your gentle heart. You saw something in my face — longing maybe. And wanted to comfort me."

Ann nodded. She couldn't speak. But Rachael could. "I guess I'm not like a lot of mothers-in-law."

"That's for sure. And thank goodness!"

"I've not speculated or even thought about when or whether you should have children. This is a personal concern. Even now my first thought was, 'We must take care of Ann, David and I.' "

"That's like you."

Rachael leaned over and picked a white clover blossom. No fragrance was sweeter. No wonder bees use it for making honey.

"How do you feel about this, Ann?" Rachael asked.

"Happy — and also a little scared. I've observed a lot of children *and* parents. I'd not want a baby to be just a doll or an extension of my ego. I'd want it to be an individual — a cherished and distinct identity."

"Then it will be," Rachael said. "Sometimes I've thought that young parents worry too much about what to do or not do. Read too many books. If they have the right values and aims what they do will have good results."

"You think so?" Ann asked.

"I do. I remember how I felt when David was on the way. I wasn't excited or couldn't plan on how things would be. It, the baby, seemed unreal until I really knew him. Saw him learn, grow, and display his own characteristics. Then I ached to keep him as God made him. *And* I don't think I did a bad job."

Ann smiled. "I agree. Oh, Rachael, I'm so fortunate to have David and to have you for a friend."

They went back to the group. Rachael wondered if the glow in her heart showed on her face. David soon reminded them that they should leave by four in order to be home in time for the youth group meeting.

She was glad to be home. The day had brought surprises. She needed a quiet time to assimilate the happenings. She changed into a checked gingham dress and comfortable shoes before going outside for a stroll around the house.

The moss rose bush was embroidered in tightly rolled pink buds. And the pin cushion blossoms of the snowball bush were turning from pale green to white. A whip-poorwill's call came from somewhere beyond the elder-berry bushes across the road.

There was a kind of harmony all around her. The sky blended with the earth through the fringe of trees on the horizon. She'd heard a minister say that Indiana was the only place he'd been where the skyline was bordered by trees. The soft light of evening was matched by the hushed call of the birds.

Suddenly, a wave of Sunday evening loneliness flooded her thoughts. She had a half a notion to go up to Til-da's after she'd had a bite to eat.

She'd made a slice of cinnamon toast and a cup of tea when a car turned in the barn lot gate. *I don't know anyone with a car like that.*

Within a few seconds she saw Tilda and Kenneth Holden coming up the back walk. She brushed the crumbs from her fingers and hurried to open the screen door. "Come in. Come in."

"I'm filling in for the Cedar Creek pastor tonight. I can't stay, Mrs. Brooks," Ken said. "But I'll leave Mrs. Barley and come in later if you don't have other plans."

"I don't and I'm glad you brought me company."

"Well, I coaxed him to come down to my place for hot cakes and sausage, then begged a ride," Tilda said. "Sunday evenings seem longer than most, somehow."

"I know. I truly know."

128

18/

As Kenneth started the metallic gold car, Rachael said, "Did he have trouble? I mean is that a borrowed car?"

"Oh, no. It's his," Tilda said. "You hadn't heard?"

"No. David hinted that Brad James was working on an idea, but that's all."

"Well," Tilda said. "Kenneth didn't say much. But I gather that he and Mr. Laine worked out some kind of arrangement. Ken's going to pump gas a few hours a week now and more when he's out of school. But I've got a feeling there's been some secret giving in this deal."

"Sounds like it," Rachael said. "But the plan seems good. Kenneth's alone most evenings. Say, what are we doing, standing out here? I have chairs."

"Are you too leg weary to take a little walk up the Macedonia Pike?" Tilda asked.

"No. As long as we don't go too far."

"Well, I thought I saw cranes down along Cabin Creek — this side of the patch of willows. They're real pretty birds. And we don't see them too often nowadays."

"No," Rachael said. "They've been driven out by

noise and traffic, I suppose."

"My, but the elderberries smell good," Tilda said as they rounded the bend. "Seems like they're bigger down here."

"Probably so," Rachael said. "Their roots aren't so far from a source of water."

They stopped on the bridge and leaned on the iron railing. The water was clear. There'd been no rain to stir it up for over ten days. The moss on the smooth stones was bright green. Silvery minnows darted in the rippling stream and circled around a log which had fallen slantwise into the water.

The two friends talked softly while keeping watch for the snowy, long-legged cranes. Rachael sketched the happenings of her day, leaving out the news that she was to be grandmother. This was for Ann to tell. Then she said, "It seemed like the attendance at church was up even if Sam wasn't there," she said.

"Yes. It went over the record attendance by ten," Rachael said.

"When was that record set?" Rachael asked. "Easter?"

"No. Further back than that. Last September. Homecoming Sunday, I think."

"I remember now. This Easter didn't bring much new life to Willow Bend," Rachael said.

"There," Tilda whispered. "See the crane down close to the floodgate."

"It looks so fragile," Rachael said softly. "On account of the long slender legs."

"There's another," Tilda said. "Coming from the tall grass. Do you suppose they have a nest somewhere near?"

"I don't even know where they build nests," Rachael

said. "My curiosity's aroused. Let's look it up when we get back to the house. As she turned she caught a glimpse of the cornfield up the road. Plowing had been finished and the ground cultivated to a mealy seedbed. Now, rows of green corn marched across the brown soil. By the Fourth of July the crop would hide the earth which nourished its growth. Long-leaved plants flourished in the row which had been sharp and ridged.

Rachael turned on the lamp as soon as they walked in the living room and she and Tilda talked until Kenneth came back. They felt the same about Sam Clinton's absence from his usual place in church.

"It didn't seem right," Tilda said. "I've been as put out with that man as anyone. There have been plenty of times when I wished he'd learned the meaning of the word no. But he's a part of the fold. It wouldn't be Christian for him to be shut outside."

"Of course *he* decided not to come," Rachael said. "No one asked him to stay away. No one would."

"That's true," Tilda said. "It's his pride and his strong will. Do you reckon he'll *ever* come back?"

"If I know Sam as well as I should, he will. It's hard to say when. But I hope something or someone gets him to come soon. The longer a person stays away the more likely it is that they'll never come back. Like Lottie Springer."

"Lottie?" Tilda said. "What brought her to mind?"

"Well, it's a kind of long story," Rachael said. "Some of it only Lottie should reveal. But she's going to prayer meeting with me tomorrow night."

Tilda didn't respond to this news as Rachael expected. "You don't seem surprised."

131

"No. I'm not — not overly," Tilda said. "I've seen Kenneth in the store several times and Lottie mentioned that he'd ridden to town with Art a couple of times when they needed things from the wholesale house."

"You think Kenneth has had an influence on the Springers?"

"On them and a lot of others," Tilda said. "You know, Rachael, I've had the feeling lately that Willow Bend was ready for a minister like him. Someone who'd move and act as if there weren't two factions."

A hard-backed June bug flew toward the window and thudded against the wire screen. The evening breeze stirred the wisteria vine and it brushed against the side of the house.

"I think you're right, Tilda," Rachael said. "An aggressive man would have stirred up one side or the other. We had the other kind."

"The mealymouthed type," Tilda said.

"Of course there's another way of looking at this," Rachael said. "We were probably ready for someone like Ken who'd lead us in a way most were willing to follow."

"True," Tilda said. Then she leaned over and untied the knot in her brown oxfords. "These shoes aren't broken in yet. A little tight at the instep."

"I noticed you had new shoes. They look nice."

"Yes. I'm getting to be quite a spender," Tilda said. "But it doesn't seem so reckless, now that something's coming in."

Rachael asked if she'd missed anything special by leaving before Sunday school. Tilda said that the only thing was the naming of committees for the homecoming.

"That's months away," Rachael said. "Kenneth seems to

be thinking pretty far ahead."

"Well, at least he's thinking," Tilda said. She went on to say that Lucy Cavanaugh, Cora Landess, and Rachael were on the program committee. "Do you think you can be an umpire if those two come to blows?"

"Do *you* think they'll even serve together?" Rachael asked.

"I saw something that makes me believe they'll try. As I walked up the aisle I heard Lucy say, 'Then you'll call Rachael about getting started.'"

"They were *talking?*" Rachael asked.

"Some. But I haven't told you everything. Kenneth announced another committee, named a cochairman. One's Brad James."

"And the other? It couldn't be — "

Tilda smiled. "It could and is. Sam Clinton."

"I wonder if he'll accept?" Rachael said.

"It's up to him. He's included."

The minister came back a little after nine. "I didn't maneuver to bring you together," he said. "But I've been wanting to tell you my news. I'm having company next month from Detroit and from beyond Wyandotte."

"Your aunt?" Rachael asked. She'd risen from the couch. "Don't say any more until I get back. I'm going to get us a glass of lemonade."

"Sounds pretty good," Ken said. "My throat's been in use a lot today."

"Ours too," Tilda said.

The minister was a little shy as he went on to tell about his visitors. Or was he touched?

"Aunt Esta has rented a van," he said. "You know, one with beds like a camper."

133

"She could stay with you now that you have the open-out sofa," Tilda said.

Kenneth took off his glasses and rubbed his high forehead with the palm of his hand. "You don't know my aunt. She's probably never made an improper move in all her life."

"But she's your aunt," Rachael said. "What would be — "

"It's because of Judith," Kenneth said. "She's the girl I may marry *if* she likes what she sees here."

"And she's coming?" Tilda said.

"Yes. She's going to drive. He went on to tell that Judith Lozier was an elementary teacher who was taking a summer workshop at Wayne State University.

"We broke up when I came down here," Ken said. "Judy's always lived in the city. Besides that she's one of a big close-knit family, likes her teaching job, and she was pulled two or three ways I guess."

"But now she's coming down to look us over," Rachael said.

"Yes. She kept on going out to see Aunt Esta to check on me I guess. Then she began writing again."

"Was it your idea to have her here?" Rachael asked.

"No. It might have been my aunt's though. She's wanted to come and she likes Judy."

"Well," Tilda said. "I sure do hope Willow Bend is on good behavior."

Kenneth stretched his legs out. They reached almost a third of the way across the room. "I just hope Judith sees this place as I see it."

"And how's that?" Rachael asked.

"As a haven — as a fruitful field — as a place where

people have gentle souls and kind hearts and a kind of tempered and controlled wisdom."

Rachael and Tilda looked at each other in surprise. "You can say all that about us?" Mrs. Barley said. "You can't be blind to the feuding and fussing."

"No. Not blind," Kenneth said. "I knew about the trouble before I came. I was warned and cautioned and advised. No one could have followed all the advice I heard. It was confusing and conflicting. But I was lucky. On my first day in Willow Bend I was given a nudge, a clue."

"You were — who said what — or should I be that nibby?" Tilda asked.

"No one said anything — at least the first person I met didn't. I've often thought that the flat tire I had that day was a fortunate occurrence."

Rachael's face felt warm. She knew what Kenneth was about to say.

"I walked into *this* room that day," Ken said. "Mrs. Brooks told me she thought every minister should be allowed to see things through his own eyes. That led me to realize that my attitudes and actions should be God-directed not adjusted to people."

Rachael's mind was flooded with humility. She'd been aware before that one remark could have wide influence; as a pebble thrown into water started widening circles of waves. But she'd never thought of her own words as being especially effective. The text "Let the words of my mouth, and the meditations of my heart, be acceptable in thy sight" assumed immediate and bright significance.

Tilda's eyes were filled with tears. She had to clear her throat to say, "There's another side to that story. It wasn't only you that didn't hear about the fuss from

Rachael. She's kept mum about the whole mess."

"I'm not the only one," Rachael said. "There are others — like you, Tilda. We've seen what was happening and didn't know what to do to help things — only be still."

"The reasonable remnant," Kenneth said thoughtfully. "I've heard that expression several times. Theoretically it sounded good but in practice — it's — well almost miraculous."

"That's what you meant the prayer circle to be, isn't it?" Rachael said. "A gathering together of that part of the congregation."

Kenneth nodded. "Right. But I had no idea of how much power there is in a small group working together for good. Sometimes I feel well tingly, or almost electrified."

Suddenly Tilda tilted her head toward the door which opened on the front porch. "Did I hear thunder?"

Kenneth got up quickly. "If it is, I'd better go. I left the window open above my couch."

Rachael followed them to the side gate. The night was dark. Churning black clouds hid the moon. A wind was rising and the leaves of the cottonwood tree in the barn lot, which rustled in gentle breezes, now rattled like dry paper. A streak of lightning zigzagged in the sky above the barn.

She went around closing windows and shutting doors. The air was cooler and freshened even before the first big drops pelted against the windowpane.

Rachael lay down on the couch to review the day. She didn't want to go to bed. Either Ann or David called after thunderstorms to be sure everything was all right.

The lamp cast a mellow circle of light over her chair, the footstool, a section of the rose-beige rug, and one end of the bookcase. She heard the refrigerator motor click. The rolls of thunder diminished and the shower slowed to a pattering. It hit the tin roof on the kitchen, like miniature castanets. *That sounds pretty — silver castanets.*

She felt herself drifting into sleep. And words, "my doctrine droppeth like the gentle rain," came to her mind. It was a quieting thought — comforting — soothing — blessed. . . .

Epilogue

WILLOW BEND HOMECOMING PLANS SET

The twenty-fourth annual homecoming at the Willow Bend Church, southeast of the city, is to be observed September 25. Former pastors, members, and friends are invited to come for the regular services. A basket dinner will be served at 12:30 and the afternoon program will begin at 2:00.

Bradley James and Samuel Clinton are cochairmen of the event. Mr. Clinton advises people to park in the lodge hall lot. The church yard has been graded and newly seeded.

The Author

Dorothy Hamilton was born and still lives in Delaware County, Indiana. Her years of elementary and secondary education were in schools in Cowan and Muncie, Indiana. She attended Ball State University and has taken professional writing courses and work by correspondence from Indiana University.

Mrs. Hamilton grew up in the Methodist Church. She was active in school, community, and church activities until the youngest of her seven children was married. Then she was led by prayer-induced direction into the activity of being a private tutor.

This, in a real sense, is a mission of love. More than 250 girls and boys have come to Mrs. Hamilton for gentle encouragement, for renewal of self-esteem, and to learn to work.

The experience of being a mother and a tutor is the inspiration for much of Mrs. Hamilton's writing.

She is the author of *Anita's Choice, Charco, The Killdeer, Tony Savala, Jim Musco,* and *Christmas for Holly,* has sold thirty-four serials, fifty-five short stories, and several articles to religious publications since February 1967. She has also written for radio and newspapers.

Seven of her stories have been accepted by quarterlies, including the *Ball State University Forum.* One story, *The Runaway,* was nominated for the American Literary Anthology.